CEO

Who suspended engineering!

Written by

Neeraj Jain

Title of the book: CEO

Copyright © Neeraj Jain

Edited and typeset by Neetwee
www.neetwee.com

This book is a work of fiction.
Names, characters, places and incidents are either a product of the author's imagination or are used fictitiously. Any resemblance to actual people living or dead, events or locales is entirely coincidental.

Written under the Neetwee Story

Lots of love MOM and DAD.

Love you Mr.AkhileshTiwari (CEO News Bindass)
Mr. Devendra Ausar (CEO Divine Infosec)
Mr. Khomendra Deshmukh (CEO Khabar Warrior).

Life Belongs to them Vishal Baharani, Nidhi Jain, Riya Patel, Garima Patel, Lekhram Patel, Harshad Dewangan, Mohan Patel.

Edited by   Mayank Gajpal.

Special Thanks To   Shruti Chandrakant Balve
Harshad Dewangan
Ankita Jaiswal.

Published and Distributed by NotionPress

Produced By Neetwee

Love You MUMMAA...

Today there was a discussion in every corner that one of the top IT company B-TECHNOLOGY was totally ruined.

The owner of the B-TECHNOLOGY company denied to meet the news-media but they were standing right in front of the office.

There was a lot of dispute ongoing about this company in the news channels from quite a few days.

News- The good days of "B-TECHNOLOGY" are over or say the company itself is completely destroyed.

No members of the group of directors have been talked to us yet, but there is no loss of any employees of this company. And there is a news that one of the company has taken over the shares of B-TECHNOLOGY along with all the employees of the company.

Yes! We are talking about WE-TECH company, which is just 4 years old and has jangled over the whole world. WE-TECH is an educational media company which is based on solutions to all the students. WE-TECH is a company whose founder is unknown.

On the other hand, the financial supporter of B-TECHNOLOGY or say because of whom the company runs, "The Director Of Institute of Engineering and Science, MR. AJAY SHETTY", has not given any statement to the media against this matter and when the media approached him, his reaction was very normal as if he didn't care. Who knows whether it is all power of becoming a god or just a drama.

FEW MONTHS BEFORE

Institute of Engineering and Technology, MUMBAI

At Director's Office

Director - Ajay Shetty.
Sir was working like his normal days. After sometime he took a little rest and just when he opened the website of WE-TECH on his system reading about some technical issues, his secretary was on door. He asked, "May I come in sir?"
Director sir - Yes Vinod, come..

Then again sir started doing his work and staring at the website with full concentration. Meanwhile, the secretary was keeping some files on the sir's desk. Sir told him to remove some files from behind from the shelf.

Vinod - Yes Sir.
Then Vinod went behind to remove the file and started looking at sir's laptop and said while giving the file, "sir this is WE-TECH, the all rounder company in the world."
He continued, "I have heard that worlds biggest IT corporates are buying the shares of this company and social sites have tie ups for educational pages too.

The thing to think about is that it's been just 3-4 years that this company has opened and it has given a tough competition for a company like B-TECHNOLOGY.

But nobody could meet the founder of this company yet. Some say that he doesn't come in front of anyone but keeps in touch through telecommunications and takes the help of his agents.

Director Sir – "Oh great! You know a lot about this company but you are not paid here for your general knowledge." sir said this to Vinod in an angry tone.
Then suddenly sir threw all the files kept on the table angrily and told Vinod to get out of the college and never to show his face ever again.

Vinod - "Sir please forgive me. All the students also study from this and recently there has been a lot of discussion on WE-TECH. That is the only reason I spoke about it. Please forgive me." He requested a lot to the Director Sir.

Director - (shouting more angrily on Vinod) "Get out I said!!"

Then director sat alone in the office and Vinod left the office.

Director then started speaking with himself.

"I won't leave you WE-TECH's owner. I will find you out from any corner of the world and ruin you. I'll make sure

that you are destroyed. I will see you founder of the WE-TECH. There will be some or the other way to destroy you, your company and I'll put an end to this name."
Director was very tensed as he had put all his money to buy the shares of B-TECHNOLOGY company.

2 Years Before
ENGINEERING BEGINS

At Institute of Engineering and Science, Mumbai

One student was coming running from the college gate. He was thin and too skinny. He saw two boys walking in front of him and thought that they are also students, might be seniors. They too were going towards college building.

He shouted at those two boys, "wait sir, please wait." And the two boys stopped and turned back.
They asked him what had happened and why he stopped them.

The running boy apologised and said, "Today is the first day of the college. So I just wanted to know if you could tell me where the first semester class is ?"

They said, "no, first tell your name."

That student said, "Sir, my name is Anil. Now could you please tell me where the class is? I'm already running late."

They said, "abbe, tell your full name. Anil what...? Kapoor???"

"Sir, it is Anil Sharma. Sir class please?"

They asked him why he was late.

Anil - Sir I woke up late and then there was a big queue for the toilet.

The two boys asked further whether he went to the municipality bathroom for bathing that he had to stand in line.

Anil - No Sir. Not bath. I went to flush out my tummy. Not in the municipality but hostel bathroom and then when I went to have a bath, the water got over.

The two boys started giggling and then one of the boy asked him whether he did his toilet proper or he left all efforts to be used there only for his studies.

Now Anil got very irritated and yet again he asked them for the classes.

Both of them then teased him and said, "Now you are late beta.. And as we are your seniors, get ready for your punishment."

Anil - Means ragging Sir? It's wrong Sir. I was just asking about the class.

One of the two boys then said, "shut up you fool. First you get late and then argue with us. Now stand still and we will do the needed."

Anil - sorry sir. Ok. Do whatever you'll want to but just remember that I'm not gay. So do according to that please.

They said, " just shut up, we are also boys. Do you feel we are gay? U fool."

Anil – "No sir. Actually, you said you would do whatever you want, so I just predicted."
One of the boy said to the other boy, that this Anil is too much and we need to do something about this. He asked him for a chalk.

Other boy gave him the chalk, " here it is, bhai. Take."

Anil was standing there itself while they were passing the chalk.

Then one of the boys said, " Now I will teach you a lesson."

Then he drew a circle around Anil and said, "you will stand here till another thirty minutes and won't come out of this."

Anil - But sir, I'm already getting late for the class. And I just had asked you for the class only. Please let me go sir.

Two boys - Again class! Why are you so much behind the class? Are we troubling you or you are troubling us?

Anil - But sir anyhow I have to go for the class after 30 minutes. So tell me for that at least.
One of the two boys -" he is actually right." Said to other boy.

Further he said, "Do one thing, when you'll be standing here for 30 minutes, think nicely and if you see anyone then ask them."
Anil - No. I will think myself and won't ask anybody else again.

Then the two boys went ahead laughing and said that they might come anytime so don't move and if anyone asks then say that Mr. SHARMA has given me the punishment.

Anil - Ok sir.

Then Anil kept thinking and realised that he has been trapped and he won't ever ask anything to anyone.
And on the other hand, the two boys went towards their class laughing and giggling.

The names of the two boys were Prakash and Mayank.

Prakash said to Mayank while walking, "See Bhai, your dream of annoying someone is complete now and we had lots of fun too. Right na?"

Mayank - True. You are right, bhai. Now what to do next?

Prakash - Oye, Bhai! Now it's my turn to complete my wishes and you have to help me in that.

Mayank - Yes Bhai, I know that. And you know I'm always there with you in everything. Now tell me fast what is our mission going to be.

Prakash - I didn't think of that yet. Wait for some time, let some ideas flow in my mind. We will now attend our class. We have already got late because of that guy and anyways it is Mr. Sharma's lecture. He is always upset on us. So let's go fast.

Mayank - yes, you are right. Let's run.

AT CLASS ROOM, 1st SEMESTER,

Mr. Sharma was taking the class, just then Mayank and Prakash entered the class asking, MAY I COME IN SIR?

Sir - (looking at both of them) "oh you two are late again!?? Oh wait no! No problem. May b we have started the class a little early today also. You both are on your time. It's all our mistake. Right?"

Mayank - no sir. When did we say so. We were just saying that this won't repeat again. Sorry sir.

Sir - when is this next time going to come my son, please tell me. From last two weeks you are telling me the same thing. Is there something written on my forehead?

Mayank - yes sir. There is something.

All the students started looking at Mayank, Prakash said slowly to him to just shut his mouth.

Mayank - No Bhai. Just wait. Let me talk to sir... Sir if we ignore the late part, then isn't our attendance 100%? Yes right? That means we are attending your classes consistently from last two weeks even though we are late. And that we didn't study even a little but we respect you, that's the reason we attend your classes. You are only not understanding our love for you.
Mayank said this all to Sir in one breath and everyone in the class started staring at him and Mayank started taking long breaths.

Sir - aare stupid! What is the connection between this and what is written on my forehead? Let it be now. That's not needed. I came to know what you can see on my forehead after listening to all your stupidity.

Now listen to me, believe me or not, it is my love that without shouting on you, I'm making you stand outside class. At least some time come early to my class you idiots. You are even removed from the hostel just within a week. I have heard that u bursted a bomb on the television set there. Poor warden, was raising the volume of the songs, could raise to just one point. Till now he is taking the treatment for his ears. If this is your love, then please keep it away from me son.

Now if you come early from at least one student, only then you'll get an entry into my class. Now go and come early tomorrow then at least any one student.

Mayank - Ok sir.

Prakash - wait Mayank. Sir, you said we have to come early then at least one student only then we will get the entry. So sir we will wait here today and I'm very sure that you will take us inside the class and there will be at least someone who will be more late than us.

Mayank - (said slowly to prakash) What are you talking Bhai. Who will be more spoiled than us here?

Prakash - aarre you just shut up. Did you already forget Anil?

Mayank - oh yes!

Prakash - ok sir. We will wait outside the class. Thank you.

Sir - try your luck. Nobody will come. I don't think so there's more stupid human born other then you and if possible, maintain silence at least for my love otherwise please leave the college if you can.

 Mayank - Sir, but...

Prakash - Shut up man! Are you crazy? Sorry sir. We are waiting outside.

After this they both went out of the class.

After leaving the class, both the mischievous boys sat on the floor outside the class. Mayank said, "Bhai this Anil will come na? Otherwise we won't get to sit in Sharma's class from tomorrow."

Prakash - I'll see how he won't let us sit. But you don't even study then why are you crying like Sharma's wife?

Mayank - It's not my fault. I just have one confusion that how these studies are useful further in life. That's the reason I don't study and skip it. Believe me when I'll know the usage of education, you will see me struggling a lot.

Prakash - Oye illiterate! Why are you hitting me? Didn't you find anybody else?

Mayank - People say there is nothing greater than a friend and there's no happiness greater than friendship. That's why I have chosen a friend like you.

Prakash - Yeah yeah! You might even trade me someday. Just shut your mouth now. Otherwise I will break your face.

Suddenly, prakash realised. He said, Bhai, we have told Anil to say that he was punished by Mr. Sharma. But if he comes here and sir asks him why he is late, and he tells that Mr. Sharma had punished him then we will be dead.

Mayank - It is your fault. I had told you to check the time table. If we had told Pandey sir's name then we would have got saved.

Prakash - You just keep quiet and let me think. If we run from here then sharma wont let us inside the class and if Anil doesn't show up then also he won't take us. We are stuck!
Then Prakash started staring at the floor. Guess he was thinking something.
Mayank - Bhai...

Prakash - Eh donkey! Please keep quiet. Why are you eating my head?

Mayank - But bhai?

Prakash - I said to keep quiet na..

Mayank - Ok fine. Don't say anything to me later.
At that time Mayank wanted to tell Prakash that Anil is coming towards the class and he might see them both.

After that Anil came in front of them.
Oh sir! Why are you here?

Prakash saw up and got a little shocked.

Prakash - and Anil.. You here? What happened? Didn't you find your class yet?
 " Sir, this is my class."

Prakash - no. This is section B. You might be in A section. A for Anil, go that side, go-go.
No sir. I had gone to the department. One of the sir took me there. He showed me the list. This is my class. Ok sir. Now I have to go. And yes sir, I have stood for 30 minutes there. Ok sir. Byeee..

Prakash, Mayank - nooo Anil...

And Anil entered the class.
Both Prakash and Mayank started thinking and both knew that they are trapped.

Anil - May I come in?

Sir was drawing laser emission diagram on board when he entered. And angrily Sir turned towards the door and asked him, " Who are you my lord ??"

Anil - Sir, Anil singh.

Sir - Why didn't you tell me your pin code? I would have come to your house to teach you engineering. Why did you take the trouble?

Anil - Sorry sir, may I come in?

Sir- You are too early for this class, so please get out.

Anil - But sir I am outside the class itself.

Sir- Shut up. Stand outside with those two idiots.

Anil - Two idiots?? Means? Are they both from this class?

Sir- Of course. What do you think they are?

Anil - No sir, but..

Both Prakash and Mayank were listening to this conversation from outside and they both knew that they are trapped.

Then,
Sir - (to Anil) speak, what happened? What but???

Anil - Nothing sir, sorry. I'm standing outside. Next time this won't repeat.
After hearing this, Mayank and Prakash got a sense of relief. They were happy that Anil had saved them.

Then Mayank and Prakash peeped inside and said to sir,

"see sir, we had told you, that there will be someone who will b more late than us. So now please let us inside."

Sir - oye! Stand there only. Just 5 minutes are left now. You want me to give you highlights of the class now or what?

Mayank - No sir. Only attendance is enough.

Sir - You people stand quietly outside and I want to see 3 of you tomorrow in class.

Anil - Ok thank you sir.

Mayank and Prakash - Yes sir, they said with a dull face.

Till then Anil had realised that he was been fooled by both Mayank and Prakash.

ONE DAY IN CANTEEN

Mayank and Prakash were sitting in the canteen. While sipping cold drinks, suddenly Prakash asked a question, by flipping the bottle of cold drink.

Prakash - Bhai Mayank, I have heard that Kasaab was given an AC room by the Government.

Mayank - Was he studying in our college? Then why there is this biasing with us?

Prakash - Arre stupid! I'm talking about The Ajmal Kasab.

Mayank - Why brother, Is he kasab's father? Is he from the same college? I never thought that this college is so old.

That's why I guess the toilets stink a lot here, they must be 100 years old by now.

Prakash - (Prakash started staring angrily at Mayank) oh please forgive me. It's my mistake. I won't ask you any questions here after. Sorry. I didn't know I would do such a big mistake asking you this.

Mayank - No worries brother. Don't take it on heart. I'm there na. You don't take any tension. I'll find out who Kasab is and his father too. You just relax and don't take stress.

Prakash - Yes brother. Please find out and keep the information with you only. Don't tell me. I won't ask you any questions from today. God knows why I got stuck here. I'm leaving. Bye.

Mayank - Aarre! Bhai, at least drink your cold drink.

Prakash - No. Let it be. I suddenly started hating cold stuff.

Mayank - But bhai..
But Prakash left from there telling Mayank not to come behind him asking on the same topic.

Mayank - Is this something from your wishlist? Anyways it's your turn to complete your wish list.

Prakash - Yes brother it's this only. Now please go. It's your turn now. Forgive me.
Prakash came out of the canteen and thought to himself that he had to sacrifice one wish cause of that foolish Mayank.
After coming out he sees a group of seniors circling around the new boy, Anil.

He felt that they were trying to trouble Anil so he started keeping a watch on them.
He got to know that they were ragging this new boy and asking him to put his shirt-off his body. They were 3 seniors in total.

They had surrounded Anil and were constantly troubling him.

Prakash got angry seeing this and he rushed towards Anil. While going ahead he raised his voice saying, "please let him go."

Seniors - Why is he coming in between? Let it be. Let him come. We'll see him too.

Prakash - Please sir, let him go.

One from seniors - why? Why are you so itchy? Wait. Let's remove your shirt too and a little powder will take ur itchiness away.

Prakash - Please sir, I'm telling you in respect. Leave him.

Senior - You are doing a lot respect respect. Wait we'll tell you how to respect us. Go catch him tightly.

Then they grabbed Prakash's hand and when he tried escaping, another senior caught his neck and said now enough of your drama. You have done a big mistake by coming here.
Anil started apologising and requesting them, "sorry sir, please let us go. I'm sorry from his side too. Forgive us."

That time Prakash had become too furious and he was staring at all the seniors very angrily.

Senior noticed Prakash and said that this guy is very nasty, take them to the bathroom.
Seniors dragged them both towards the bathroom.

Prakash was in anger but he walked with them as he wanted to save Anil from them.

Seniors started pushing them from behind and took them both together.

While they were moving towards the bathroom, Mayank saw them and sensed something was wrong. Then he also started walking behind them.

After that seniors along with Prakash and Anil entered the bathroom and Mayank came to know that something is going to happen.

Seniors locked the door from inside and started troubling them both. "now say what were you saying? You were jumping a lot outside. Now what happened to u? Come on. Let's remove their clothes guys."

Prakash was boiling with anger but couldn't do anything and Anil was tired pleading and apologising with them.

Suddenly there was a noise behind the door. "who is it?"

"Open the door, I have seen you people taking the juniors inside forcefully and troubling them. Come out otherwise be ready to get suspended."

Seniors got scared thinking it's some professor who saw them and that they are dead now. They said to the two boys, "we will see you two later."

Prakash started laughing slowly and told them to open the door and see.

Seniors said in rage, "why you stupid? Is the professor standing outside your father?"

Prakash - you'll know it when you see it.

Then seniors saw slowly through the door just then one of them said, "I guess this are relatives of some big professors. We should leave from here."

Then seniors said sorry and then they let them go from there.

Meanwhile another voice came out behind the door, " open the door fast!"
Seniors got too scared and came out and saw one of the senior Sir from mechanical department standing there. They got too scared and started saying sorry and told sir that this won't repeat here after.

Sir - What are you even saying? And what were you three doing inside being boys? Go run from here.
Seniors - sorry sir. Thank you for forgiving us.
And they went away from there.

Sir started thinking about why they were apologising to him. Then he started searching for that boy who made him stand there. These boys are really weird. He said and he too went away from there.

That time Prakash and Anil were hiding inside. Then they came out when all left and Mayank too came and gave a hi-fi to Prakash and asked him how was it while hugging him. Prakash said, "well done brother! Had fun."

Till then Anil was standing besides in a puzzled mind thinking what really happened!

Prakash and Mayank looked at him and asked, "Why are you so quiet and shocked?"

Anil - the day I joined college, something or the other is happening and it is all because of you two people. And whatever happened just now is out of my knowledge.

Mayank - wait. You'll know it. Let me explain to you. It's just that I and Prakash have a strong connection and whenever one of us is in trouble another comes to the rescue. And if we don't come, then there is no meaning of this friendship.

Anil - I still didn't understand.

Prakash - You crazy! If you want to tell him, tell properly, why are you simply making it complicated and telling your own philosophies? (said to Mayank)

Mayank - see brother. I'm telling him, so let me tell. Don't disturb in between. Yeah, so where was I? Okay, listen.

When the seniors were troubling and hitting you both, one of my friend called me and I was listening to all the conversation on the phone. After that secretly I followed you people.
Suddenly, Prakash - oh you idiot! Tell me straight. And when was I scared?

Anil - Oh brother! You are so smart!!

Prakash - Thank you.

Anil - what happened next brother Mayank? Who shouted outside the toilet? And where did the Sir come from?

Mayank - It was me who shouted from outside but then I thought if they come out, I'll get caught. Just then I saw one of the sir going by and called him near me.

Mayank - sir, excuse me.

Sir - yes, what happened?

Mayank - sir I need susu.

Sir - what?

Mayank - sir I mean I want to go to the toilet please.

Sir- so then what? Do you want to take my permission in front of the toilet or do you want me to open the zip of your jeans?

Mayank - Yes sir. I want you to open.

Sir- what rubbish are you speaking?

Mayank - sir listen to me first. All what I meant is opening the door. I guess it got stuck in between. I tried but now I can't even control and no more strength.

I acted so well at that time that sir really felt that I'm urging to go to the toilet.
And when sir started pushing the door, I was standing right behind him and that time seniors must have felt there was some professor who is pushing the door outside angrily.

When sir was busy knocking and pushing the door I slowly escaped from there without him noticing me and I hid behind. Just after that the seniors opened the door. So this is the story.

Anil - Great brother. You are so smart and intelligent.

Mayank - Thank you friend. This isn't anything great. I have done much more than this.

Prakash - Oye don't get excited. He is not praising you for your acting, he is just saying thanks to you for saving him nothing more. Now come on, let's go from here.

And you, Anil, if we are done with helping you, shall we leave? You go and do your studies.

Mayank - What are you speaking? What has happened to you?

Prakash - Look bro. I had to help him. I did it. Now it's done. Over.

Mayank - Let's do friendship with him. Anyways he is alone. Poor guy.

Anil - Yes Bhai.. Can I stay with you people?

Prakash - No. Not at all.

Mayank - What are you speaking Prakash bhai? And Anil you can stay with us,from today. You are our friend, Our Bhai.

Prakash - Mayank, don't talk like a psycho.

Mayank - I'm not acting weird. It's you. What is your problem? Why are you doing so much of drama?

Prakash - See, don't force me more.

Anil - Sorry brothers. Please you people don't fight. I just asked casually. Sorry. I'm leaving.

Mayank - whatever you are doing is not right Prakash. There is no logic in this.

Prakash - See Mayank, it's not about wrong and right. There is some other reason. Forget it now.
Mayank got a little upset and tried to stop Anil who was walking away. Prakash too was standing there but he didn't go near them. Mayank started talking about something with Anil alone.

Mayank - Anil bhai. You please don't take Prakash's words on heart. I really don't know what's wrong with him today.

Anil - No brother. I'm fine. I just simply asked it. Don't worry. I guess he's better with you only and he must not be willing to spend time with anybody else.

Mayank - No brother. There's nothing like that. We both are normal.

Anil- What normal? I can see that you both know each other very well and you guys be happy with each other.

Mayank - It's nothing like that. We are boys only.

Anil - Yeah! That is there. But u guys are special for each other.

Mayank (raising his voice a little) - Bhai, we are boys only and there is nothing between us like you are thinking!!!

Anil - wWhat did I say?

Mayank - See. We are both boys and good friends too.

Anil - Yeah.. I know. You both are special for each other.

Mayank- No anil, you are thinking wrong.

Anil got very confused and after thinking for a few moments he said, "what wrong did I say? I guess you are taking it wrong. I was saying something else."

Mayank - That's what. Anything you are speaking. We are not gay.

Anil (shockingly) - Gayyy??? What are you speaking my friend. I was talking about the pure bond of friendship. You are speaking nonsense.

After saying this Anil started walking back and Mayank started saying sorry bhai, my mind is... Sorry sorry. I started thinking about something else.

Mayank - OK. Listen, we are friends from today.

Anil - What drama is this now?

Mayank - Yes Bhai, I'm serious.

And Mayank hugged Anil.

Anil - Thank you Bhai.

Mayank - Hey! I will break your head. Never say thank you to your friend.

Anil - Sorry.

Mayank - Arre! No sorry too.

Anil started smiling and told Mayank that his friend Prakash will be upset with this.

Mayank - don't worry about it. I'm the biggest tension for him. He'll soon agree to this. Now let's go for the class.

Anil- class? And you?

Mayank - yes. Let's study something.

Anil- good to hear that from you.

Mayank - we have to go to the physics lab.

Anil - do you like this subject?

Mayank - no. It's nothing like that.. Actually my net pack is over and lab gives you free WiFi and you get good range too.

Anil started laughing again and asked him whether he was this way always?

Mayank - it's difficult I know. (he said with a naughty smile)

Physics Lab

In the lab, Mayank tried to talk to Prakash and told him that Anil is a good guy and be good to him.

They both were talking very softly to each other.

Prakash - i know that he is a good person. So what do you want me to do? Make him a bad person?

Mayank turned to the other side and saw Anil. Actually Prakash, Mayank and Anil, all three were standing in the same row. And Mayank was standing in the middle.
He was trying to talk to both standing there.

Mayank - Please Prakash, tell me what is the matter?

Prakash - Why are you after me? Everything is alright.

Mayank - No. Its not. Looking at your mood I don't feel things are right.

Prakash - No it's nothing like that and now don't disturb me. Let me study.

Mayank (staring at Prakash in a weird way) - Whom are you trying to fool my dear? First of all this is lab. And I know you come here just to use WiFi and download movies, that too those MMS. And you are holding a maths book in your hand just to hide your phone inside. Atleast u can tell me what's the matter? Tell me, you know we don't hide anything from each other. Friends don't hide anything right?

Prakash - I never win from you. But please don't disturb me now. Let me download the video and you too download something nice. Don't talk now. If sir sees us, then he'll make us clean the whole lab later.

Mayank (in a happy tone) - Now that's like my friend .

At that time, Anil was listening to their stories and he felt good that he's in between such good friends and he had noticed that these two guys cannot stay without each other.

Suddenly Mayank saw Anil and asked him where he is lost? And what he's been thinking about.
Anil- nothing at all bhai. Just like that.

Mayank - anyways, now you are a part of our gang Anil, now Prakash also won't say anything. Just let his MMS download now.
Anil started laughing.

AFTER SOME DAYS

Before the examination of first semester in college.

Anil - Bhai, exams are starting from the next few days. What to study? I just want to pass this semester any how.

Mayank - This is something great about you intelligent people. You haven't failed any test yet and you are scared for the exams. Look at me, I haven't passed properly in any of the tests. Think what will happen to me. My parents will kick me out of the house and then I'll have to die as an orphan.

Anil - You stay outside the house only then how can anyone remove you out of the house? And nobody becomes an orphan after being removed from the house. Don't talk rubbish.

Mayank - Bhai, these are emotional feelings which intelligent people like you won't understand.
A boy named Shubham from class comes in there.
He asks Anil for his help.

Shubham - brother, one program is not getting implemented. Can you please help me with this?

Mayank - Hey you stupid? Do you think we are software engineers? Go and catch some computer science or IT student.

Anil - Mayank, you shut up. Sorry bhai. He is mad. He doesn't even know the spelling of Engineering till date. Don't mind him.

I'll come in the class and then help you with it.

Shubham - Ok thank you bhai.

You dumb! (Shubham said to Mayank)
Anil started laughing and teasing Mayank after that.

Mayank - Oh please. Shut Up now.

Anil- Okay sorry. Tell me where is Prakash? Can't see him anywhere.

Mayank - He has gone to remove tickets for 3 of us.

Anil - Tickets? What kind of tickets? And why am I not aware about this?

Mayank - Bhai, even I didn't know. All this happened today morning.

Anil - What happened?

Mayank - When we were sleeping, Prakash suddenly got up and said let's go out to explore.

I told him that exams are nearer. But he said right after exams, next day we are going out.
I said we'll see.

Anil - But what exactly happened?

Mayank - Actually it was Prakash's turn in mission khwaish.

Anil - So?

Mayank - So he said that it's his dream to go out to goa after exams.
I told him that it's not possible and asked him to tell that it's just this semester that we are going out.

So then Prakash said, "that's a good idea. Now my wish is that we'll go out after every semester exam and nobody will say no.

Mayank - No bhai. Please don't say that Anil too will accompany us.

Prakash - This is also a very good idea. Now 3 of us will definitely go and this rule is fixed for us.
When Mayank was telling this story to Anil, he shouted, "Mayank are you out of your head?"

Mayank - No dear. I just have a bad stomach.

Anil - Shut up. I'm not talking about that. You dragged me also simply in that plan. I won't spare you now. Not just for one semester but for entire engineering.

Mayank - Sorry bhai. But I didn't tell him to do anything.

Anil(In temper) - You didn't say anything but u gave him a boost for his nonsense.
I won't go anywhere with you guys.

Mayank - No bhai. Don't say this. Prakash won't spare me.

Anil - You deserve that.

Mayank - Bhai please. Think. We are going to goa.

Anil - So what? Can we go to goa for free? Or shall we walk? Or do your father owns a hotel there??

5 Days After

Anil- Because of you guys I have to go to goa in such a short notice. Firstly you'll woke me up at 6 in the morning and blocked both the bathrooms. It was better if I had come directly from the hostel only. Simply I stayed with you people yesterday.
You people didn't even let me have bath nor to do potty. God knows what you people were doing inside the bathroom.

Mayank - Why are you getting upset Anil bhai? You do your stuff on the way somewhere. There's nothing to worry about. Chill.
Anil - Hey you brainless! What you want me to sit down with a bisleri bottle roadside stopping the bus? Don't talk like your retard face.

Prakash - Why are you getting so upset? Okay sorry. We'll buy you a tumbler somewhere from goa then you search for a place as per your comfort.

Anil - Now you just shut up okay. It's all because of you. You never get ideas to attend any class but you used all your energy to plan for goa.

Prakash - Ok sorry. I was just kidding.

Mayank - Yes my friend. I'm sorry too. But you make your mood proper.

Anil - It's okay. There's no need to say sorry. But don't tell me to come anywhere next time.
Prakash and Mayank - next timee...!!

Saying this they both looked at each other and started laughing.

At hostel, after the exams of fourth semester

Prakash and Mayank - Wake up Anil.
(slowly they both tried to wake Anil up)

Anil was sleeping, he was taking a rest after his exams were over. Even after them trying alot Anil didn't get up. Mayank emptied one bottle of water on him.
Anil got up in a shock and was surprised to see Mayank and Prakash in his hostel room that too so early in the morning.

He asked them what they were doing there and why they threw water on him.
Mayank - it's not water, its my susu.

Anil - What??? You stupid people. I won't spare you both.

Prakash - No yaar. He is telling you any nonsense. That's not true.

Anil - But why did you wake me up? And how did you both get into the hostel? If warden sees then he will throw you both out and me also. You people have already been thrown out in the first semester itself. Now let me live in peace here.

Mayank - Oye keep quiet. And listen to us. We have an idea.
Anil - Yeah so you should called me from your Idea. I have airtel. Why did you come here with your sick face?

Prakash - Oh please stop your stupid stuffs. And get ready fast. Idiot. We have come here
crossing your hostel boundary hiding from the guard then climbed up through your balcony.

Anil - What? Are you people crazy? What was the need to do all this? Are you going to get some award doing this?

Mayank - We won't get anything. But one of our friend was hiding here in the hostel. So we came to take him from here.

Anil - Ok now stop being so emotional. And tell me what work you have.

Prakash - First get ready at least.

Mayank - We have a surprise for you.

Anil went to the bathroom to get ready.

Prakash - Ready Mayank?

Mayank - Yes. All set.

Prakash - Now pack his bags otherwise he'll do a lot of drama again. And remember to leave some of the clothes here.

Mayank - Yes I'll do it. You just keep an eye on him.

Prakash - Yes don't worry. I'm standing near the bathroom only. I'll signal you the moment he comes out. And listen, we can't take the bag in front of him so throw it out of the balcony once you are done with the packing. Then we will collect it while leaving.

Mayank - Ok. That's all fine. But what signal will you give? Do one thing. Shout "bachao bachao."

Prakash - Oye! I'm not getting raped to shout bachao bachao. I'll do one thing. I'll shout saying Su-su. Ok. I'll leave now.

Then Prakash went near the bathroom and Mayank started packing Anil's bag.
Mayank was very much in a hurry to collect his clothes and pack the bag. He started putting all the clothes from Anil's cupboard into the bag.

An on the other hand, Prakash was standing outside the bathroom. After few minutes, one guy from the hostel came and stood behind him. He started looking at Prakash from behind. Suddenly Prakash turned back and got scared and shouted su-su.
And here Mayank felt Anil is coming so he got nervous and pulled out all the clothes and even a jeans and a shirt kept on the bed and threw the bag out from the window. That was the back portion of the hostel.
And on the other side,

Prakash - Oye! Who are you? And why are you standing behind me?

Boy - I'm from this hostel itself but I don't think you are. What are you doing here?

Prakash - me?
Prakash started thinking and looking up and down. Then he said,
"I have come here to do su-su. I stay there besides. That bathroom is not working so I came here to use this.

Boy - There is no bathroom there because there is no building besides this hostel nor any house. There's only one playground.

Prakash - Yeah. I mean,..

Boy - What do you mean? You stay on the road? This stupid warden, I don't know why he let's some beggar's inside the hostel?

Prakash - Oh hello! I'm not a beggar!

Prakash started talking very loudly and so Anil could hear his voice inside the bathroom and he came to know that his friend has created a scene outside.
Anil came out of the bathroom wrapping the towel fast. He asked the other boy coming out,

Anil - What happened Bhai?

Boy - Look sir, this warden is allowing any random roadside people to use our hostel bathroom.
Prakash got furious and said, "again you said the same thing to me??"

Anil started calming down Prakash. He told him to forget everything what he said.
He told the other boy that Prakash is his senior.

Boy - Senior?
He got scared and apologised to Prakash,
Seeing you I didn't feel that...

Prakash said cutting his words, "please shut up now."

Anil - Let it b yaar, he is new to the college. How will he know that you are his senior?

Prakash - What if he is new? He can't call anyone a beggar just like that?

Anil - Leave it yaar now, he got mistaken cause of your face.
And there Mayank was thinking about what was going on outside. He wasn't going out because he had made a big mistake there. He was thinking what to do next.
There Prakash was telling Anil,
"oye! My face is proper ok. You look at yours. And that fellow, his face looks like some shit. I won't leave him now." (he said pointing out at that guy).

Then Anil told Prakash to go in the room.
Then they both went into the room but the moment they entered the room, they saw Mayank sitting very tensed on the bed.

Prakash - What happened to you now? Why you are sitting like all your energy is drained?

Mayank - Yes my friend. All energy is gone.

Prakash - Means?

That time Anil was opening his cupboard to remove his clothes and suddenly Mayank shouted coming in front of Anil, " no brother, don't open. Nothing is left in this world."

Anil - I'm opening my cupboard you idiot, not 'zindagi na milegi dobara.' "
"please stay aside and let me take my clothes out."

Mayank - They are out already!
Prakash was listening to both of them.

Anil- Out means?

Mayank - They fell outside.

Anil - Ehn? How can they fall just like that from the cupboard? Please wait let me see.
And he pushed Anil and opened the cupboard.
But the moment he opened it, he was shocked and numb.

Anil(looking at the cupboard) - What is this? Where are my clothes?

Mayank - They are out there. I told you na. I packed and threw them out of the window.

Anil(in anger) - But why?? What bad had I done to you?

Mayank - Sorry yaar. Actually I and Prakash thought you won't agree to do this. So we decided to pack and throw your clothes in a bag and then run away from here along with you.

Prakash - Bhai. He must have not thrown everything away. I'm sure he must have kept some.

Anil - Yaar. What kind of plan is this? Does anyone plan of taking their friend this way? Looks like you have come here to run away with your bribe along with the property.
Anyways. Give me some of my clothes. Anil said calming down a little.

Prakash - Yes of course! Mayank, give him his clothes.
Mayank started looking here and there.

Anil - Give my clothes!!! Now what you want me to beg for it?

Mayank - Bhai, please ask someone for it.

Anil & Prakash - Means?

Mayank - I threw all the clothes out.

Anil & Prakash - Whattt??? (both said at the same time)
Anil - you stupid, idiot..

Mayank - if you don't know any bad words then its okay. I can understand your feelings.

Anil - Just shut up.

Prakash - I had told you to leave some clothes na. Why did you throw all of them?

Mayank - guys, you people were all fighting outside, so I thought you are coming inside. So I got scared and threw all of them out.

Anil - So now what do I wear?

Mayank - Ask someone to give you something to wear for now.

Anil - Why should I wear someone else's clothes. I won't wear.

Mayank - Ok wait. We'll go and get your clothes which are thrown out.

Prakash - Oye you brainless! We have climbed 8 feet up and you have to throw the whole stuffed bag down. How will we climb with that? I'm surely not coming for any help. You have done it so you only go and get it.

Mayank - Help me out yaar. Please

Prakash - Not at all. Go alone.

Anil - Do one thing. Take any guy from the hostel. Let him be here.

Mayank - Ok bhai.

Prakash - What okay? If anyone comes to know that we came up climbing the wall and they tell warden then?

Mayank - Nobody will tell. We Engineers are true to our words.

Prakash - Heyyy! Engineers are also known for their crazy and weird behaviour at times.

Mayank - So what to do? You are not going to come, can't take anyone else. So then?

Then Mayank looked at Anil and said, "there's only one way left now."

Anil - Why are you giving me that weird look?
Mayank - you have to run this way only . And now I'm also not in a mood to go and get your clothes and stuffs.

Saying this Mayank sat on the bed.

Prakash - Yes my friend. Now u decide. There is no other way too.
Prakash too sat on the bed saying this.

Anil - Stupid, idiot....

Mayank & Prakash - It's ok bhai, if you can't give bad words. We understood your emotions.

Anil – "What to do now? Tell that at least" he said angrily.

Mayank - Told you na. There's only one way. Run with us.

Prakash - Yeah right! Go out and wear your clothes. Anyways, nobody comes around the back side of the hostel building.

Anil said some very harsh things to both of them in anger and started walking.

Mayank - Take your mobile along with you if you are leaving.

Anil - Why don't you throw this away? Now where do you want me to put this? In my underwear??

Prakash - Please calm down both of you and think about how to go.
Then they opened the door and searched to see if anyone is around. Nobody was there out. So they started running.

Anil - What's the matter? Why everybody is in their room today?

Prakash - We know what all you hostelers do inside your room.

Mayank - Bhai. Stop innovating this MMS in your mind and get going.

Three of them came down safely.
Anil - Mayank go and see if the warden sir is sitting there in front. Go slowly, and just peep and come.

Mayank - No. I'll go and sit and drink some alcohol with him. Stupid. This much brain I also have.

Prakash - Now be quite you both, and Mayank, please go fast and let us know.
Then Mayank went to check and came back soon.

Anil - What happened?

Mayank - Our path is clear brothers. Warden is outside and he is looking in the forward direction. I think we should go from behind now, i don't think he'll come.

Prakash - That's great. Let's go.

Suddenly a voice came.
"where are you going?"

Prakash – "Aarre!! We'll go out." he said looking at Mayank

Mayank- Bhai. I didn't ask that.

Prakash - Oye! Let's go outtt! (this time looking at Anil)

Anil - Bhai, I too didn't ask.

Prakash - what? Then who was it?

Anil & Mayank - look behind.

Anil - now my fees are going to go in water.

Mayank - Think in this way that you won't have to eat food from here anymore.

Prakash - What are you guys speaking?

Saying this he turned and the time he turned he became quiet.

Now,
Anil, Prakash & Mayank - warden sir, you here?
All three said this together.

Sir - Yes son. I'm here. But you two are removed from the hostel long back. I guess now you'll came to take somebody else with you both. Anil beta, I guess you won't be able to stay here now.

Anil - Sorry sir. (he said in a crying tone)

Sir - No son. I'm sorry.

Anil - Sorry sir. (he said with more crying expressions)

Sir (shockingly) - That's all fine but what are you doing in towel Anil?

Anil - What to do sir? Now I have got such friends, so had to come out this way only for them.

Sir - Great son. Maintain your friendship nicely. But please come to the office too. Let's nicely roast your friendship more.

Suddenly Prakash - Sir, look there behind you.

Sir - Who is it?

Sir turned back to see.
And in a second Prakash removed Anil's towel and threw it on sir face and ran so that sir gets distracted.

But Anil didn't move and he was alone left there. He didn't even realise that Prakash removed his towel and threw it on sir.

Prakash came back running and pulled Anil along with him. Everyone started running. Anil was annoyed with all the things that were happening with him. He started saying things to Prakash and Mayank.

Mayank - Run faster. Warden is behind us only.
Sir (while running) - stop you three idiots.
Prakash - Not today sir. We'll see you some other time.
All three ran towards the wall and climbed and crossed it.
Sir went till the wall but couldn't cross it.
Then three of them flew from hostel. They took Anil's bag and kept running so that nobody could catch them.

All 3 stopped somewhere after sometime. They were breathing heavy. They all looked at each other and started laughing.

Then Anil – You made me run in my underwear. And started laughing again.

Mayank - It's good na. Your clothes didn't get spoilt in sweat.

Prakash - We should get some Oscar or something. Whenever we 3 are together something or the other interesting has to happen.

Mayank - Yes brother. That's absolutely true.
They started laughing again.

Anil - You people have made me an orphan now. Tell me where will I stay now?
Mayank - Why? Our room is there na.

Prakash - Yeah. No Sunny Leone is going to come there. So you come with us.

Anil - It would have been good if Sunny Leone was there.

Prakash - Yes beta! Don't you think you are hoping for too much?

Anil - What kind of place are we standing in? I guess this is the garbage house. It's stinking so much here.

Mayank - Yes. This smell is bad.

Prakash - First you wear your clothes here Anil.

Anil - Yeah, that's fine. We'll see what to do next.

Prakash - Yes. Then we'll go home and Mayank it's better we tell him our plan there itself why we got him here this way.

Mayank - Yes bhai.

While talking, Anil started putting on his clothes.

At Room of Mayank and Prakash

When they reached the room,

Anil - What the hell is this yaar?

Mayank - This is our house.

Anil - It's so dirty. It's even more dirty than that garbage house.

Prakash - Whatever and however it is, now its your house too.

Anil(said slowly) - Can't do anything now. Had to leave the hostel because of you people. Can't go back there. Go order something to eat. Till then we'll clean a little.

Prakash & Mayank - Clean up??? (they asked shockingly)

Anil - Yes of course. All have to do.
Then they ordered some food and did cleaning till then.

Prakash - So we are leaving tomorrow right?

Anil - Where?

Mayank - Forgot his wishlist?

Anil - No. Now it's not possible. Forgive me you both.

Prakash - Oye!! Let's go na. We'll have a lot of fun.

Mayank - Yes. Don't act now.

Anil - I don't want to go anywhere.

Mayank - We'll decide for some place now only.
Suddenly Prakash got a call from his classmate and the
moment he picked up the call, he was shocked.

Prakash - Hello.

Friend(on call) - Did you see the notice? We have got a msg
from college.

Prakash - What happened? Is the director dead? I didn't
open the messages. I was a little busy.

Friend - It's not funny. I'm serious. Director sir won't leave
us now. He has called us in the college tomorrow.

Prakash - Is it something urgent? Because I have a plan of
going out.

Friend - You always have a plan. I won't tell you everything
else now otherwise you won't come tomorrow. Meet me
tomorrow, I'll tell you.
And he kept the call.

Prakash - Hello... hello..!

The call had already got disconnected.

Mayank - What happened?

Anil - What happened? Why did your face turn yellow?

Prakash - Soorry guys. The trip is cancelled. Director has called in the college tomorrow.

Anil - Yessss...!! (screamed in excitement)
Mayank and Prakash stared at him in rage.

Anil - I mean! Oh.. No!! That's sad.
Mayank to Prakash - No worries bro. It's just a matter of some time. We'll leave after you come or may be the next day.

Anil - Yeah. Don't take any tension. But I'm getting tension now.
Mayank and Prakash again stared at him angrily.

Anil - I meant to say. We'll surely go. If not today then tomorrow, else day-after-tomorrow.

Mayank - You don't take any tension Prakash bhai. Think about it in a good way. At Least we got some more time to plan and decide where to go.
Prakash - Oh yes yaar. I didn't think only about this. Ok chuck it. We'll think about that tomorrow.

Anil - okay. So let's sleep for now.

* Some time later *

Anil was sleeping in between Mayank and Prakash and suddenly he opened his eyes.

He heard some dangerous voices. And when he looked here and there, he realised it's Prakash and Mayank who are snoring very loud.
Anil was stuck between them.
He couldn't sleep properly the entire night.

Next Day in College.

Mayank, Anil and Prakash reached college. Prakash ran towards his friend Sanjay who had called him the earlier day.

Prakash - What really happened that you couldn't tell me on the phone yesterday?

Sanjay - Sorry my friend. If I had told you on phone then you wouldn't have taken it seriously and bringing you to college today was important.

Prakash - will you please tell me what happened?

Sanjay - Director has called the entire college in the hall. I have heard that he is going to announce some project competition.

Prakash - So? What do we do? We are not even good at our studies.

Sanjay - That's not important. Actually everybody's presence was important. There was a notice on the college website and I was sure you wouldn't read it.
And then there was some announcement on the speaker.

Speaker- all the students now have to come into the hall of the college, Director wants to notify something.

Sanjay – Here is the call. Let's go.

Prakash - Ok fine let's go and see what happens.
Prakash called Mayank and Anil and they walked towards the hall.

At Seminar Hall -

All the students were present in the hall and after some time the Director of the college Mr. AJAY SHETTY and the Principal of the college Mr. DILIP GHARDE came along with
some of the members of the management. Professor Sharma was one amongst them.
All the students and the faculty stood up.

Director - It's just a matter of few minutes so please keep standing. There's no need to sit.
I'm going to tell you something very interesting, which might be dangerous for you or can be beneficial as you are getting a chance to prove that you are an Engineer.
When I was a student like you, I had a bad habit to come top in the college. I was so much dedicated to my studies and to top that I never missed the chance of coming first. Not just that but also maintaining a constant first position of this college in India. And I promise that till I'm here, I won't let anyone change this position ever.

My Professor once told me, Ajay, Engineer is not just a student, but he is a warrior, it's your pride. If you are an Engineer, then never let this pride go down anytime. You can bring anybody else down but not yourself.

Director said with a smile, "Thousands of Engineers came and went here, some were unsuccessful, some became tired and got suspended, but I didn't let this engineering college die. I supported this engineering system throughout."
And to maintain this and expand it further, I'm going to take another big step. Today I'm announcing " BE ENGINEER " competition.

There was a sudden noise in the hall as everyone was curious to know about what this competition is all about.

Director - Please be quite. Let me complete first.
As per the rules, to participate in the competition, a student will have to register his name first, and they will be given a time of exactly 2 months. You all must be thinking why this time and what all you have to do. The participants need to submit a project and it will not be the projects like your exams need, this will be a huge one.
I will be personally approving all the project or say your technical invention and it should be the one that will make the name of our college shine.
So even a minor mistake is not acceptable here nor things which are copied. If participants are found with any such projects, he will be disqualified. And not just this, but he will even be suspended from his semester exams.
Listening to this, all the students started talking about it and there was noise again in the hall. Most of them got scared. Because of the fear of suspension, most of the students decided not to participate in the competition.
Director - Pay attention students, you will participate in this competition in groups and maximum 3 in a group. But please be careful, the group who will be participating will register his/her name on the college website till today evening and tomorrow morning their names will be announced here by me.

One of the student - Sir, may I?

Director - Yes, please.

Student - Can a group have members from different branches?

Director - Yeah definitely, all are engineers, after all.
After that all the students left the hall.
After coming out,

Prakash - This competition is not our cup of tea brothers. We should stay away from these things. We can't study properly for semesters only.

Mayank - Yeah. You are right bhai.

Anil - So what now?

Prakash - Now what? Forgot? We have to leave for our trip. Has anyone thought about the place? We forgot that in this confusion. Anyways now we are away from all this.

Mayank - We'll do one thing. Let's go to the canteen. We'll decide it there. Anyway, we haven't had anything these days by taking the bill on the name of Sharma sir.

Prakash (laughing) - Okay. Yes. You said it right. Today Sharma will pay double money.

Anil - Why do you guys simply trouble and irritate him? Poor fellow.

Prakash - no faculty is so good. They just want to give some burden to students. They think we are their labourers. They don't stop giving the assignments. Sometimes I feel to take the revenge of their graduation they graduate others in a wrong way. They don't have any good intentions. Otherwise which teacher says that you won't be able to study this? They are so discouraging. They are the reason why India is lagging behind in development. What is less in us? We do all the efforts. Now you tell me, can anybody be more mischievous than us in this world?

Mayank - bhai bhai, it's ok. We got what you are trying to say.

In Canteen

Anil, Mayank, Prakash and his friend Sanjay were all sitting together in the cafeteria. Prakash ordered 4 plates of samosa in the name of Sharma sir.

Anil - yaar Sanjay, this registration is there only till 4 pm right? Then when will the results be out?

Sanjay - I don't know anything properly yet but I guess we all will be called in the seminar hall again in the evening. You people don't think of running away from here at all and please drop the plan of going anywhere today. Anything can happen, so sit in the college quietly.

Prakash - Oye! But we have a plan of leaving for the tour today.

Sanjay - Bhai, if Director sir gets angry today then you will have to permanently go on a tour from the college.

Mayank - I don't know why sir is so serious with this competition. I can't find any of the students interested in this.

Sanjay - That's what director wants.

Anil - Means?

Sanjay - I have heard teachers discussing about it and even our seniors that director is doing all this cause of that WE-TECH.
Anil - WE-TECH? that educational company?

Sanjay - Yes. I think sir is annoyed because of that company. Actually in the same market, sir is having his own investment company B-TECHNOLOGY, whose situation is worsening because of this WE-TECH.
I think sir is doing this to keep up the market status, so that people get back their attention to B-TECHNOLOGY company. The results of this contest will be decided along with the B-TECHNOLOGY incharge. Director wants a bigger technical market with him then WE-TECH.

Anil - Umm.. But how do you know so much about this?

Sanjay - I feel so, that's just my opinion.

Mayank - It's so complicated. I'm not understanding anything. Anyways, why should I be bothered, let the director sit and worry about it.

Sanjay - I wish it was so easy. This is Ajay Shetty. You don't know but he can do anything.

Prakash - Sanjay, what we don't know? We didn't get what you are saying.

Sanjay - How will you know? Nobody knows I guess. This story is too old. What Ajay Shetty had done years back, I hope that same time doesn't come back now.
Anyways leave that, it's none of your use.

At 4pm Evening

Mayank, Prakash and Anil were in the college campus when some students came and called them to come inside the seminar hall where sir was going to announce the participants names.

At Hall -

All the students gathered again and the director too was present there.

Director - We have got the names of some teams who are going to participate in the competition.
So now I'll announce the names one by one.

Group 1- Sidhesh Maheshwari, Rajesh Mehta, Sanjana Kothari.
Please clap for them.
*all the students started clapping *

Group 2 - Ashish Meshram, Sanju Singh, Alka Tiwari.

Group 3 - Pankaj Adhikari, Kanha Agarkar, Anjana Desai.

Don't stop clapping. And now it's the last group. This group has registered on the last moment on our site and we are happy that they took the right decision.

Group 4 - Prakash Rathor, Anil Singh and Mayank Gupta. (and this time the entire hall kept clapping, and just 3 amongst them were standing still without clapping)

Prakash, Mayank and Anil were shocked hearing their name and thinking how it was possible that their names were announced without even registering.
After this everybody started leaving the hall and Prakash screamed loud in anger, "who has done this nonsense? Have any one of you done this?"

Anil - I haven't done it.
 Few moments later sanjay reach to them an d said " have you guys gone mad? Why did you give your name? you know the rules right? If your project got rejected by falling under cheat or copied you all will be suspended from the semester.
May be that is the reason beside of thousand students only few of them participated in this stupid competition."

"you guys wanted to prove yourself genius or fool" said sanjay again.

Prakash- Sanjay, we have not done this, we are trapped.

Sanjay- I don't think that anyone have that guts to do so otherwise director would punish him first.
Mayank- bhai, what can we do? We could be destroyed.

Anil- Our engineering, my life could be destroyed and we can't do anything.

Prakash- I know , what to do. Sanjay just a minute. You two come with me.

All three went to the director.

Sir was walking on corridor and prakash called him from behind.

Prakash- Excuse me sir.
Sir- Yes, say.

Prakash- In the competition, we didn't. I mean we did not...(Prakash was not be able to say anything clearly.)

Director sir- Say whatever you want, I don't have whole day.

Prakash- Sir we didn't participated in the competition.

Sir- Did not participated means?

Prakash: Sir In the last group our name was announced but no one of us has given the name. So sir please rule out us from the competition.

Sir- Rule out...?

Mayank- but sir really, we didn't give the name.

Sir- Is it a joke, all of you are fools. Nothing can be done just go hell out of here.(sir shouted on them).
After saying this sir started walking and all of the three were upset. Prakash thought to request again.
Prakash- Sir please listen. (Prakash said from behind.)

Director Sir turned back and slapped him on face. "Go get lost from here. Don't come behind me. Now you just have one way either to participate in the competition or leave the college permanently." and he left.

Prakash (crying) - We have been trapped sir. Please believe us.

Mayank and Anil came running and took care of Prakash.

All three were very tensed. They were walking out of the campus.

The three sat on one bike. They were very tensed and tired thinking what to do next. Sanjay saw and came near them.

Sanjay started explaining them and told to participate in the game.

Anil - If we come to know who pushed us in this problem then you see.

Prakash - Don't worry bro. We won't leave him. You don't take any sort of tension. Nothing will happen to us.

Anil - So what to do now?

Sanjay - There's one way actually. It's a bit weird but it's better than what will happen to you later.

Mayank - What is it Sanjay? Tell us fast.

Prakash - yes sanjay tell us. We can do anything to get out of this situation.

Sanjay - There is one boy. Don't know where he is but professors which are old will surely know.

Anil - There is no tension about that. Sharma sir is there na. We'll take it out from him. But what's the thing?

Sanjay - There is one big story in college related to him. I have heard that he was very intelligent and very brilliant student. Call him super genius. We say such people have God's gift. He was that type. But director had removed him out of the college insulting him in a very bad way. But I don't know the reason.

Prakash - Aarre are you mad? Why do you think he'll help us, for what reason? And how old story are you telling us? How is this related to this matter? We don't want to fall in anybody else's matter.

Anil - But brother, we don't have any other way.

Mayank - Yes, exactly. We are trapped from all the sides. Please Prakash bhai, try to understand.

Sanjay - See. I had told you first only that this will be weird. But he can totally help you in this. And now to save yourself you just have one way. Search him. Rest all is your wish. Think about it. Okay then. I have to go.

Prakash - Ok bye.
Then Sanjay went.

Prakash - Listen, we are not going to step in this another problem. We are already having lots of problems. To search him, get him here in all this we will simply waste a lot of time.

Mayank - But understand the situation and think at least once.

Anil - Yes yaar.

Prakash - No yaar. I don't want to fall in another trouble and I don't want you both to fall in this. I'm going to the room now. You people come.
Saying this he went to the room.
Anil and Mayank were very tensed.

At Room, Night:

All 3 were tensed and scared since evening and were sitting on the terrace. They felt they have spent all their engineering life in having fun and roaming and enjoying and now they are getting the punishment of what all they did.
They started crying and were too scared.
After some time, Mayank went near Prakash and Anil also came the same time and both stood in front of him.

Prakash (said very emotionally) - What happened? Why did you come like this to me? (Prakash was again and again hiding his face and talking. He was putting his head down or seeing sideways while speaking)

Mayank - Nothing will happen bro.

Prakash - What happened to u? What are you saying? This is just a competition. We are not removed from the college yet.

Prakash again hide his face.

Mayank - Bhai I'm there na, nothing will happen.
Prakash hugged Mayank and said, "I promise nothing will happen to us yaar. I don't want to get out from college."

Mayank - Nothing will happen you donkey. Who knows, our life might change after this competition and everything will be fine.

Anil - Mayank is right Prakash.
Mayank called Anil closer and they all hugged each other.
After some time,

Prakash - We'll go to search for that guy and won't leave that Director too. And in this that guy's revenge will also be complete.
We'll find out about him tomorrow only. Who is he? Where is he? Hope tomorrow we'll be able to talk to Sharma sir.

At Morning, College
Date : 10 July 2017

Three of them reached college but Prakash was still feeling that they were doing it wrong taking somebody else's help. He felt that they didn't need to take the help of anybody else. And doing this would be wrong.
But he was scared thinking any wrong step would spoil the life of his friends along with him. Prakash spoke to Mayank and Anil about this.
When they were in college, going towards the class,

Prakash - Brothers, I wanted to talk to you both.

Anil - Yes say na. Anyways, God knows what's wrong with you since morning. Your face looks like a shit.

Prakash - No guys. I'm serious. I don't know what we are doing. We are trapped in a college matter and here we are going to search for a fourth person. This is really our foolishness and I don't think this is right. It doesn't even seems logical.

Anil - We know whatever you are saying is right. But we don't have any other solution.

Mayank - It's all our fault. We should have stayed properly, studied well and at least should have been honest with our engineering.

Anil - So what to do now? Nobody will listen to us even if we request them now. Remember na what Director did yesterday to us. Let's go and meet Sharma sir first. He might help us a little.

Mayank - Yes bhai. That's right. And Prakash, if you feel we don't need to search for someone else then we are with you. If you are saying there is no logic behind this, then there won't be any.
They went to Sharma sir after some time. He was in his cabin. They took permission from him to come inside.

Sir - Come inside, you three.

Anil - We wanted to do one request to you sir.

Sir - I know what you want to say but I cannot help you in this matter.

Mayank - But sir we didn't even say anything yet.

Sir - Your scared face itself is saying that you don't want to participate in this competition and want to remove your name which is not possible. Director is very strict with this matter of competition. If he comes to know about this then he will remove you from college right now. It's all up to you now. Stay in the competition and save yourself or get ready to walk out of the college. The gate is anyways open for you guys. Your wish.

Prakash - Sir, but what do we do? Help us please.

Mayank - Yes sir. Please help us. We are not able to understand anything. We tried to take help from others but it wasn't useful. You know Sanjay from Mechanical Department na? He told us to search for one boy, god gifted genius.

Sir - God gifted genius?
Mayank - yes sir. He told us that there was a guy whom Director sir removed from the college. He can help us but this seemed illogical to Prakash.

Prakash - Oye Mayank, shut up. Quite. (he said slowly in his ears)

Prakash - Sorry sir. We'll take your leave now. Thank you.
And they turned back and went out and suddenly Sharma sir got up and said, "wait wait."
Three of them turned back and thought what happened now.

Sir - I want to talk to you three. Do one thing, meet me in the canteen in 10 minutes.
Prakash, Mayank and Anil - ok sir.

In Canteen,

Mayank, Anil and Prakash were all sitting on the lunch table. Sir came and they all stood up and greeted him.

Sir - Sit you idiots. Don't give me so much respect in the place where you eat everything on my name. Leave. Tell me who told you guys about that boy.

Prakash - One of our classmates Sir.

Sir - What else do you know about him?

Mayank - Nothing much sir. Only that Director sir removed him from college and he hates director sir.

Sir - Raj. His name is Raj.

Prakash - But sir. This is not the solution to our problem.

Sir - There is. Your solution is in this only. Raj is a very talented personality. But his situation is very tough and your work is a small thing for him. But if you are with him, you might end up helping him too.

Anil - Help? How will we help him?

Sir - As far as I know, he was thrown out of the college very badly and he was alone at that time. If you be with him, he might achieve something from this college and the Director through you all. So, I think he will surely help you. And anyways this is the easiest solution which you have. And you always go somewhere far after your exams, go this time too. This journey will save your life. Rest all you all know.

Prakash - Yes sir. Maybe you are right. But we don't know anything about him. Where he is? How he is? Nothing at all.

Sir- See. I know his address but I don't know anything about him. But I just know that he is very emotionally attached to this place and you all might help him. I'm just not doing this for you but him also.

Prakash - Sir, you just said that you don't know anything about him, then how do you know that even he needs us so much?

Sir - I know his situation very well but not him. And I can assure you that he will surely help you. And if you want to know more about him then I'm ready to tell u. At Least whatever I know I can tell you.

Mayank - Prakash, sir is correct. We don't have any other option. And nobody else will help us.

Anil - Mayank is right. This is not a small competition, where we can buy any project and present it.

Mayank - Yes bhai. Anyways, we wanted to go out for a trip. Remember na Mission Khwaish? Well complete this journey. This will be a journey for life, who knows. Anyways it's my turn this time and nobody can say no now.

Prakash - Ok fine Mayank. Ok sir, we'll go to search for him today itself. Give us his address.

Sir - Ok then, I will do it. I will call you later.

Anil - Ok sir. Thank you.
Prakash and Mayank too thanked Sir and then they went from there.

At Anywhere To A Person
Date : 10 july 2017

One unknown place and an unknown person, which was not a part of this story but god knows what will happen next. That boy had too many tattoos on his body. Chinese words on his hands, some monster tattoo on his chest and his back had some name.
Suddenly his phone rang, he was working out at that time. He stopped and went to pick up the phone.
He picked up the call,

On phone - your work is done, you have to handle it further.

Boy- Ok, thank you.

He smiled and declined the call.
After that he went in a serious mood. He opened one door and there things were messed up. He removed one box, there was a specs kept inside. He wore it, and there were tears in his eyes. He said in anger, I wont leave u now. Time has come. This is the right time. He will have to regret. He'll regret that he did this. He will have to accept his mistakes. Now I'm going, I'll return late. You study till then and don't worry about me. Now first of all, Raj will have to die. Then whatever we want to achieve, we will. I'm leaving. You are listening to me na srishti? I'm missing you.
That time, he was talking to himself. Then he left to do what he said.

First Half Completed.

At Mumbai, Same Date (10-July-2017).

Prakash, Mayank and Anil, reached in their room and were waiting for sharma sir's call so that they can plan what to do next. After some time they got sharma sir's call.
Anil picked up the call and said, "hello sir."

Sir - Hello, Anil?

Anil - Yes Sir, speaking.

Sir - See. I have come to know about that guy and I'll tell you but I have a class now. So can't tell you everything now. Meet me at the CST at 4pm today. I'm coming with you people. And don't worry about the tickets. I have arranged it for all four of us. I will tell you the whole story there.

Anil - Ok sir, we will be there at 4pm.
And Anil declined the call.
Prakash asked him what sir told him.

Anil - Sir has called us at CST at 4pm. He will be coming with us and tickets are also booked. No worries. I just want our work to get done. That's it.

AT 4P. M. CST RAILWAY STATION MUMBAI

All three reached the station. They met Sir outside the station. They asked him curiously where they are going.

Sir - Chhattisgarh.

Anil - Yes Sir, it is the South Central. But what are we going to do going there?

Sir - I have heard that Raj stays there, in Raipur.

Prakash - That is so far Sir and where will we find him in such a big city?

Sir - Don't worry. I have his address. We will get him. And this is his photo. It's passport size. I have removed it from the college file. But your work will be done by this.
Mayank - But Sir, why are you coming with us?

Sir - Not with you stupid, I have to go to Nagpur urgently. I got some work there. I'll go till there with you so that I can tell you about him.
Now let's go. Train is from LTT station. We should hurry up.

Prakash - Ok Sir.

Then Sir walked in front and three followed him back. They went from local train to Lokmanya Tilak Terminal (LTT), and then caught their train and started the journey.

At Train

It must be 7 in the evening, Prakash and Sir were sitting face to face and Anil and Mayank were sitting side by side. Prakash asked Sir, "Sir you were supposed to tell us about Raj. What trouble is he having?"

Sir - Raj is a big story of this college, which is lost now. You know why I told you to go to him? Because you guys remind me of him. He was not so dumb and stupid like you people, but he used to do a lot of mischief and make fun and enjoy but always topped the college.

Prakash - topper…?

Sir - Yes. For the first two semesters he topped and for the next two he came second.

Anil - How second? And these are just four semesters.

Sir - Yes. Just four semesters. Don't know what really happened, but he left college after his 5th semester.

Mayank - Sir, you said he came second for the 3rd and 4th semester. Why second?

Sir - Somethings happened in third semester which he never thought would happen. Her name was Srishti. They have a lovely story.
It was late evening when Sir started to tell them their story. On the other side, there was somebody else who was going to come in their life.

At Somewhere

11 July 2017

That tattoo guy was sitting in the psychiatrist's clinic. Some time later, the receptionist told him, "Mr. Rajveer, now you can go inside."

The name of that tattoo guy was, Rajveer.
He said thank you to her in a very low voice and went inside.
When he entered inside, the lady doctor welcomed him, "hello Rajveer, come sit."

Doctor - How are you now Rajveer?

Rajveer - I don't know doctor. I don't feel good doing anything. I feel very tired and feel like leaving everything what I'm doing.
I feel very lonely.

Doctor - This is quite strange Rajveer. We have used all the therapies by now but there is no improvement in you. Do you still feel lonely?

Rajveer - Yes doctor.

Doctor - Did you take the medicine I gave?

Rajveer - Yes doctor.

Doctor - Why don't you try to stay happy Rajveer? What problem do you have staying happy? When you get out from this fear, you will find that this world is beautiful.

Rajveer said thank you doctor in a very low voice and started walking out. The moment he reached the door.

Doctor - Rajveer, what is there on your hand? Did you do another tattoo? Is this in Chinese? What is it?

Rajveer - Nothing Doctor.

Doctor - Rajveer tell me one thing, why are you so alone and quiet? Are you hiding something from me?

Rajveer again put his head down and said in a low voice, "No doctor." and he went from there.

Rajveer sat again to some roadside and started looking at that tattoo and started thinking about something. Tears rolled down his cheeks.

PAST
6 YEARS BEFORE
Institute Of Science And Management, Mumbai

3rd semester class was going on when HOD and few members from management entered the class. All the students stood up. Faculty said, "Please be seated."

Faculty - You all know, your second semester results were out yesterday. Now all know where you stand in the class. We have come here to wish the topper.

"Raj.. Raj.." Noise started coming from the class.

Sir - I guess all know who topped this time. Yes. RAJ SHARMA, topped again in the University.
All the students started clapping.
Raj sharma stood up and thanked everyone.

Sir - Congratulations Raj.

Raj - Thank you sir.

Sir - Everyone Please be quite. We have another news for you all. Today, we have a new student with us. You all must have already seen her by now. She's sitting in class, let me introduce her to you all. Miss Srishti, Please stand up beta. She's new here and because of some issues she has joined in the third semester directly. Hope you all help her.
(While sir was introducing her, Raj was constantly looking at Srishti.)

After some time, Srishti's eyes went on Raj. She saw Raj watching her and just when their eyes met, Raj turned his face.

But he was watching her in the middle but he used to hide his face whenever Srishti saw him.

Raj was following her in the campus and one day Srishti thought of talking to him.

College, In lunch time

Srishti came to Raj.

Srishti - oh hello topper! What's going on?

Raj was talking to his friends at that time, the moment he heard her voice and turned.
Raj became numb and got scared.

Srishti - Oye, what has happened to you?? Have you become Veda??

Raj (in fear) - Veda what?

Srishti - you.., Veda means, are you mad?

Raj - No.. No veda. Nobody is veda.

Srishti - From the time I'm watching you, 'tu mala ka anusaran karit aahes?'

Raj - Sorry what?

Srishti - I mean, why are you following me?

Raj - Ohh follow? Where, when and how?

Srishti - See, if I see you again behind me, then I will place your complaint.

Raj (scared to death) - Ok ji, no follow and no veda. promise.

Srishti - Good for you.

Then she went from there.

Raj continued looking at her from behind and his friends sitting besides said, "bhai, did you understand anything? She murmured something in Marathi and went.

Raj(smiling in his own) - It's such a nice language.
(he started blushing)

In Class

Everybody was sitting in the class and Raj had started sitting behind Srishti now.
Suddenly the boy sitting besides him said, "tests are starting tomorrow. I'm not able to understand anything yaar. There is no need for you to study. Without studying also you will top the class.

Raj - Shut-up man. Why are you taking tension. Leave it.
That time Srishti turned in anger and said,

Srishti - Now you also start worrying. Your days of being the topper of the class are over now. Now I'm there in the class, so you better take a little tension now.

Raj started looking at her with a smiling face.

Srishti - Oye, you are again smiling?

Raj - You don't worry. Till I'm here, I'll make sure only you top the class.

Srishti - what? Are you mad or what?

Raj - Nope. Veda.

Srishti got up from there and started walking. But when she turned back to see Raj,she saw Raj was still looking at her.

And then, Srishti looked at Raj and smiled for the first time. Raj got really happy and got up and went out in the campus and said "yes" with full excitement.

Next Day, In Test -

During the test, Raj was looking at Srishti and writing too. And when only 10 minutes were left for the test, Raj looked at Srishti, she was still writing the paper, and suddenly Raj stopped writing.

He didn't pick up the pen again after that.

Raj did the same for many exams. One day Srishti too turned back to Raj, and she noticed that before last few minutes Raj stopped writing and looked at her. She signaled Raj to write the paper. He indicated her back saying his paper is over and then she continued writing her paper.

Result Day

Everyone had crowded in front of the notice board. Everyone was busy looking at their results. Srishti reached there and saw the results. She had topped the exams. She screamed in excitement, "Yes!!"

Then she came out from the crowd. Everybody was congratulating her. At that time, she saw Raj coming. She went to him and asked, "Did you check the results?"

Raj - No. Not needed.

Srishti - Not needed means? Do you have so much confidence in yourself?

Raj - Yes. I have trust in everything I do.

Srishti - Are you sure? Think one more time. I feel you should see the results once more. Who knows, your beliefs might go wrong.

Raj - I told na. There is no need. I know the results. And yes Congratulations!!

Srishti - Arre....! At Least see once,... Wait a minute. What did you say? Congratulations?

Raj - Yeah. That's what I said.

Srishti - That means you know the results?

Raj - Yeah. I said na. I trust myself a lot. Ok then chalo, I have to leave. Cya. Bye.

Raj went from there and Srishti kept thinking about what just happened.

In class

Principal had come to the class along with the HOD. They had come to congratulate the topper. They congratulated the topper, Srishti, first and then they announced Raj's name saying that this time he is second in the class.

Raj - Yes Sir, thank you.

Sir - It's ok son, try your best again.

Raj - Yes Sir.
And then Principal sir left from there. But department's faculty were still there.

Department sir asked Raj, " What happened Raj? All the teachers said that you have done the same mistake in every subject. You have always done well in all the papers. But this time you didn't attempt the last few questions. Why is it so?"

Raj - Yes Sir. Sorry. I won't repeat it next time.

Sir - Okay. But remember, you are a bright student.

Till then Srishti was looking at Raj. She was understanding all the things by now. After the class was over, she met Raj alone.

She called him out from behind, "Raj..!!"
Raj turned, " Yes Srishti, what happened?"

Srishti - Why did you do this?

Raj - What did I do? I didn't get you.

Srishti - Now don't act! I know you did this all on purpose. You purposely didn't attempt the last few questions.

Raj - No. It's nothing like that.

Srishti - Oye Idiot! Now accept the truth otherwise 'mi tula thappad deyin.'

Raj - What? What did you say?

Srishti - I mean,... leave it…. Tell me why did you do this?

Raj - My heart said it so I did. I wanted to do friendship with you and you wanted to top the exams. And I also wanted that because I didn't want to break your heart.
Srishti - But what was the need of doing this all? (Srishti became a little emotional)
Raj - It's ok, really. I don't really care about all this. For me it's just a number really.

Srishti - Thank you.

Raj - Arree.. It's ok really, I told you na.

Srishti - Will you be my friend?

Raj - What?
Raj asked shockingly.

Srishti - Yes. Let's be friends.

Raj - Ok fine. I don't have any problems.

Srishti - Chalo - Chalo, now don't do this drama. Whole semester you have followed me, now don't show me this attitude.

Raj - ok sorry.
And then Raj took his hand forward for a handshake and said, "Hey! I'm Raj Sharma."

Srishti smiled, "Hello! I'm Srishti."

Raj - Srishti what? Tell me your full name.

Srishti - why? You didn't hear that in the class till now?

Raj - I have heard and I also know a lot about you.

Srishti - what do you know?

Raj - I know that you like singing, fighting and you are our Principal's daughter.

Srishti - Yes. So you should respect me.

Raj (laughing) - Yes of course Madam. But why did you join in between? I don't know about that.

Srishti didn't say anything. She became quiet and started walking away.
At that time Raj said something that made her wait.

Raj - 'Jevvha mi tula pahile tevvha mi fakt tula pahu icchit aahe. Aata mala fakt tujya baddal janun ghyaychay aahe.'
(that means, from the time I have seen you, I just want to see you and now all I want is to know everything about you in my life)

Raj said to himself that maybe my marathi isn't clear but my feelings are clear about what I said. But no problem, slowly slowly I will surely talk in a proper marathi language.

Srishti turned back to Raj, looked at him and she had tears in her eyes.

Srishti - Did you learn marathi?

Raj - Yes. Some few things just for you. That's it.

Srishti - But why all this?

Raj - what do we call that in Marathi? Haan yeah, Veda!! I have become Veda. I have become totally veda for you.
Srishti started crying and she hugged Raj. She started crying even more. Raj too had tears in his eyes but he was very happy as Srishti was with him.
They kept hugging each other for a long time.

Raj - Srishti, please stop crying. Tell me what happened? I'll be with you always.
Srishti wiped her tears and said sorry to Raj.

Raj - It's ok. Come with me.

Srishti - Where?
Raj - Come first.

In Canteen

Raj(with a glass of water in his hand) - Here. Have some water. And calm down.

Srishti - Thank you.

Raj - That's completely ok. Sometimes our mind cannot handle the things we have in our hearts. So we need to speak them out. That lessens our burden. Speak and see, you might feel good. And everything can change into something good, you never know.

Srishti (emotionally) - I used to stay in Delhi. I did my first year of engineering in Delhi Engineering College. After the second semester exams I was supposed to return home. It was my mom's birthday the next day. I had planned on giving a surprise for her by telling only dad about me returning home. You know, I didn't talk to my mom waiting for this day for almost two months. Actually the last time I went home, I had a small quarrel with her as she had not bought me a dress that I liked.

That time angrily I had told her that I won't talk to her from now and I went back to Delhi. That was the last day of my holidays. I jokingly said that I won't talk but then thought of doing a small drama to annoy her and always avoided her calls or lied saying I'm busy. This went on for 2 months.

Then when my exams got over, I went and got some gifts for her. I was returning home to give her a lovely surprise…. I reached home… and…,,

Srishti starts crying a lot again

Raj - Say it Srishti. Don't worry. Nothing will happen. I'm there with you.
Srishti continued telling him while crying,

Maa had left us. Leaving us here. She went so far from where she could never come back. Far from me. I couldn't even talk to her nor she could hear her daughter for one last time. It's all my fault. When I reached home, her body was kept in the house and everybody was sitting besides her. I could do nothing. Raj, nothing at all.

You know, she knew that I would come home after my exams. She had gone to buy me the same dress that I liked last time and that's why she met with an accident. Just because of me.
Srishti was telling Raj everything while crying.

Srishti - I didn't even talk to her for the last time. She used to always call me. Even went to buy that dress. I have killed her Raj. (starts crying more)

Raj immediately pulled her and touched her head near his chest and consoled her. He said, "No Srishti. You didn't. You have just loved her alot but you couldn't tell her that. Sometimes these things happen in our life. We accumulate all our feelings inside us and it's too late when we wait and delay letting it out. The same thing happened to you. You didn't do anything bad. "
Srishti kept crying. Raj too had tears in his eyes. Slowly Raj calmed her down.

After some time she stopped crying and she spoke after a while, " After mom, dad was alone here and me there. I couldn't stay in Delhi anymore. That's why I came here near dad. That's why I joined in between of the semester for second year.
Now Srishti was totally fine and she wiped her tears off.

Raj - Are you alright now?

Srishti - Yes. Thank you so much. I'm really feeling good now just because of you.

Raj - I didn't do anything. You had to speak your guilt out. Sometimes you have to betray yourself and listen to your heart. There is nothing bad in that. Who knows, it might help a lot. Shall we go out now if you okay?

Srishti - Yes.

Just when they were walking out, they stopped. They both were standing side by side. Raj looked at Srishti and asked, "What happened?"

Srishti looked at Raj, smiled and held Raj's hand.

Raj looked down immediately and saw Srishti holding his hand, looked at Srishti and smiled.

Srishti - Now let's go.

Raj started smiling again. He was very happy that they were together now.

Some time later, Raj's friend came to call him as Director sir had called all the students to the seminar hall for some important announcement.

All the students gathered in the seminar hall. After some time, Director, AJAY SHETTY, Srishti's father that is the Principal of the college and some senior faculty which included Sharma sir came in.

Director sir then announced,

"students, there is a big news for you all. You have a chance to prove yourself as an Engineer.

All the students were curious to know what Sir is going to tell them.

Director - Today I announce," BE-ENGINEER " competition. In this, you have to develop your own project and submit the research work. Then Senior professor will verify and there will be some professors from the outside multinational company in this. We cannot give you the details of the company for some security reasons nor about the judges. But this is the best chance for you as the winner will have a placement opportunity and direct interview in this multinational company. And his rest of the engineering fees will also be forgiven. That means the winner will not need to pay the fees for the coming semesters.

All the students were really happy and excited listening to this and some were scared thinking about the verification process.

Director - Registration for the competition will start from today evening on the college website. Just remember one thing that you cannot copy the project or do anything that matches the existing projects completely. If you do so, you will not only be disqualified but will also be removed out from the semester exams.

All the students were scared to participate now but Raj was happy and ready to participate.
All the students started coming out of the hall.

Raj and Srishti were together. That time Srishti asked Raj, "Are you going to participate in this?"
Raj - Yes. This is the best chance for me to get rid of some of my problems.

Srishti - Problems?
Raj - I have struggled a lot Srishti to reach here and while having no parents it is not easy. I myself have a hobby of inventing new things. I don't think I'll get a better platform than this.

Srishti - Good. All the best. I trust you. And I know you'll do your best.

Raj - And you?

Srishti - No ways. I don't want to participate. I won't be able to take out so much of time. I have to take care of dad too.

Raj - yes. I can understand. You don't need to worry. I'll win this and build our own industry. You be the boss and I'll be your manager.

Srishti- company? Of your own? You are seriously mad.

Raj - Don't you trust me?

Srishti - ok fine.. Let's walk now.
Then they both started walking. Srishti was walking ahead and Raj suddenly stopped.

Raj - Srishti, listen.
Srishti turned back and asked him what happened.

Raj - Can you meet me tomorrow? Can you spend a day with me?

Srishti - why? You want to take me for a date?

Raj - No. I want to free you from yourself.

Srishti - Free?

Raj - Yes. Today I saw a girl who needs to come out. So please. Give me your time for just one day.

Srishti - Okay. I'll call you.

Raj - Ok done. My balance will be saved.

Srishti (laughing) - "Kanjoos."

Then she started walking again. Raj kept looking at her. He couldn't take his eyes off her.

In the Evening

Srishti called Raj.

Raj - Hello!

Srishti - Hello! What are you doing?

Raj - Nothing.

Srishti - It's Ok if you are busy. I'll keep the call. Ok Bye.

Raj - Arre! When did I say so?

Srishti - Then tell me where you are taking me?

Raj - Atleast tell me first that you are coming.

Srishti - ok fine. Meet me tomorrow morning sharp at 9am on CST.

Raj (happily) - ok done.

Chhatrapati Shivaji Terminus
Srishti was waiting for Raj. Raj reached there in few minutes.

Srishti -Now tell me. Where do you want to take me?

Raj - Aare! but it's you who called me here.

Srishti - you only told me to meet you in the morning.

Raj - Yeah. But I didn't call you to the station na.

Srishti - So do you want me to go back?

Raj - Ok sorry. I was just kidding. Now let's go fast.
Then they sat in a local from CST station.

Srishti - Raj, where are we going?

Raj -Don't worry I'll tell you just have some patience.
After some time

Srishti - Raj!! You are telling me or not? Where are we going?

Raj - Come with me quietly. You trust me na?

Srishti - Ok fine but if I don't like it then 'mi tula marun takin'.

Raj - What?

Srishti - I won't leave you.

Raj - Ohh!!
Raj took her to one place.

Srishti - Where have we come Raj?

Raj - Matheran, is the name of this place.

Srishti - I haven't been here before.

Raj - There is something more special here then this. But we'll have to walk from here.
Srishti - why walk? Kanjoosi again??

Raj - This is the jungle area. Should I call for an aeroplane for you madam? Automobiles are not allowed here. No vehicles.

Srishti - Oh. But how will we go?

Raj - I told you na. Don't worry. I'm there with you. You just have to come with me.
After walking a little Srishti said something to Raj. She was mesmerised seeing this place. There were mountains on all sides and greenery everywhere.

Srishti - This is such a beautiful place.

Raj - Wait for some time. There is something more ahead.

Srishti - What more?

Raj - There is a surprise for you madam.

Srishti - What kind of surprise?

Raj - Hold my hand and come.
Both held each others hand and started walking.
After some time,
Srishti - Oh my god! I cannot believe such a place exists here.
there was a river flowing ahead which was originating from the middle of the mountain and they were at a height of 800 meters from the sea level on the top of a hill. It was a beautiful view. Srishti kept looking at it.

Raj - How's it?

Srishti - Beautiful.

Raj - Now you have to do one thing, Srishti.

Srishti - What's that?

Raj - Close your eyes and remember all your pain and fear which troubles you.

Srishti - I didn't get you Raj.

Raj - Do as I say. Close your eyes and let the pain of your heart come out.
Srishti closed her eyes and recalled some things which got tears in her eyes that rolled down her cheeks. She held Raj's hand tightly.

Raj - Now shout with me towards that hill loudly.

Srishti (her eyes closed) - Are you sure Raj?

Raj - Yes, Srishti. 1,2,3,...go.

Then both screamed to the top of their voice holding each others hand. And kept screaming loudly for a while. After some time they stopped. Srishti's tears turned into a sweet smile.

Raj - How are you feeling now?

Srishti - awesome Raj. Thank you so much. I did not feel so good before this anytime.

Raj - Now you are free from your pain, Srishti

Srishti - Thank you Raj.
Then she kissed Raj.
A cute and sweet story was given birth on this hill.

After Sometime,
While returning back, Raj said to Srishti, "you know what? Today your mom will be very happy as her daughter is now out from the dark room and that now she can love you endlessly."

Srishti was feeling very relaxed. Her pain had gone away. Now she could remember her mom in a good thought not any pain. She thanked Raj a lot for this.

Raj - I'm always there with you Srishti and you know what? I have another surprise for you.

Srishti - What is it now?

Sit in the train now, then I'll tell you.

In The Train

Srishti - Now the train has started. You can tell me now.

Raj - You like singing right?

Srishti - You want me to sing a song now ?

Raj - You have to sing along with me.

Raj started singing for Srishti in the train. He had specially written that song for her.
She was shocked seeing Raj singing for her.

They both sang together and they had a lot of fun that day. At the end, Srishti hugged Raj and they both loved each other a lot after this day.

PRESENT

Sharma Sir - So yes. This is all what had happened.

Prakash - but sir, what happened next? He was removed from the college right?
Sharma sir - Yes. He was removed from college.

Anil - But why sir?

Sir - I don't know this properly as I wasn't in college that time. But it's said that he was accused of copying the project. That too some innovation based multinational company, B-TECHNOLOGY's upcoming project.

Mayank - Sir, this B-TECHNOLOGY is the same company right which got ruined a few days back? WE-TECH has bought all the shares of this company.
Sir - Exactly. It's the same one. And I'm sure there is something about this matter. That's why I want you guys to search Raj. I know he will never cheat and may be because of you all he might get another chance to prove himself.

Prakash - And sir, what happened to Srishti??

Sir - She left the college. But where she went, where she is, nobody knows.

Anil - But sir, why are you so worried about Raj?? Why so much concern for him?

Sir - Raj was a great student. And on top of everything, he is an Engineer. Respect of an Engineer is the respect of the entire Engineering.

Prakash - Sir you know a lot about him except why he was removed from the college.

Sir - I told you na. I was out when all this happened. This was a famous story of that time in our college. All knew about it. I have met Raj, so I know him. He is a very smart guy. And he will surely help you all.

This is his address. You have to search this in Raipur. And this is his passport size photo. I have removed it from the college documents so you will have to use this only. He is not available on any social sites.

Mayank - Ok sir.

Prakash took Raj's address and he stared at his photo and started thinking about his story.

Sharma sir - Ok chalo. Now I'll take your leave. Nagpur Station has come.
Prakash, Anil and Mayank - ok sir, thank you.

Sir - No problem. From here onwards you have to handle everything smartly. I have worked here for more than 4 days then I will be going back to Mumbai and join college.
Then all three waved bye to sir from the train. Sir went and they continued their journey to Raipur.

After some hours, they reached Raipur station and started searching for the address that sir had given them.

They asked a few people here and there and reached the address. But they saw something unexpected. There was a house there but it was locked and the condition of the house was very bad. All three of them were too worried now. After this they started inquiring about the house in the neighbourhood.

Prakash asked some people nearby.

Prakash to someone..

Prakash - May I know where will find Mr. Raj Sharma?

Someone - Raj Sharma? None of this name stays here.

Prakash - But this house is theirs na?

Someone - I'm staying here from past 5 years. I never saw that house open anytime. It's simply existing there. Nobody stays there.

Prakash was shocked.

Prakash - Ok. Thank you.

Prakash told this things to Anil and Mayank. They too were shocked hearing him.
They asked some more people around but all said the same thing that they don't know any Raj Sharma. They all were too shocked and couldn't understand what to do next.

Mayank - I think we should call sharma sir. We might get some help from him.

Anil - Yeah. That's a nice idea. Wait I'll dial his number.

Anil called sir but his phone was switched off.

Anil - Bhai, his phone is off.

Prakash - Shit yaar. What is this? We are badly stuck here.

Mayank - What do we do brothers? Can't do anything here and going back also we'll have to suffer.

Anil - I think we should get out from here. At Least we can do something of our own going there.

Prakash - Anil is right. We should go back.
Three of them started walking back. Suddenly the passport size photo of Raj slipped from their hands. The man walking behind stopped them seeing the photo.

Person - Wait, your photo has fallen down.
Three turned back. That person lifted the photo and was giving it to them when suddenly he saw it and said, "Rajveer sir's photo."
They heard him and asked whether he knows him and where they can find him.

Person - This is Rajveer sir's photo. His face appears similar to this but you won't find him here.

Prakash - This is Raj. Maybe you are talking about some other person.

Person - May be. Anyways I'm talking about Rajveer who stay some kilometres away from here.

Anil - Thank you. We should move from here now.
They started walking back again.

Mayank - It's strange that, that guy saw this photo and assumed him as Raj.

Prakash - Yes, but yaar shit. This picture is 6 years old. It's possible that this Rajveer is Raj only. We might find some clue through him.

Anil - Might be Prakash. You are correct. Anyway, we don't have any other option. We have already come so far. Let's do this. But this are two different names. It's possible for the face to change in years but name? How can that change?

Prakash - Leave it. We'll figure out that later. We'll talk to that fellow who recognised him first.

Three of them turned and went back to that guy.

Mayank - Sir can you take us to this person?

Person - But he is different na? He is somebody else.

Prakash - We'll see that. Can you please tell us where we will find him?

Anil - And how do you know him? I mean that Rajveer.?

Person - He is my son's tuition teacher. He is one of the best teachers here. He teaches all the poor kids in free. He is very brilliant.

Prakash - Where will we find him? Can you take us there?

Person - Yes of course. Let's go.
They all went to search Rajveer with that person. They reached a house. That person said, "see here. Rajveer stays

here only. You might find him inside. He takes tuitions here for kids. Ok now I'll leave.

Prakash, Mayank and Anil - thank you sir. You have helped us a lot.
Then that person went from there.
Three went inside the gate. That house had a boundary wall. They crossed the gate and went ahead. To their disappointment, the door was locked again.

Prakash - What to do now? Even this is locked.

Anil - leave it. I think we should really go now. Anyways this is not Raj. What's the use of meeting Rajveer?

Prakash - You are correct but I think we should wait. At Least we'll find who he is. And his face resembles Raj. Who knows what can happen next?

Mayank - Bhai, I don't know what you people are feeling but I want to do susu. We have forgotten susu from the time we got down from the train. Even he has some rights. Respect it.

Prakash - You are right Mayank. Even I want to do susu.

Anil - Exactly guys. That's what I was thinking what I had forgotten. Let's go.

Prakash - There is some trash there. Let's do it there.
Three of them started doing susu near the trash area that too singing out loud.
While doing susu, Anil kicked Mayank from behind. Mayank's jeans got wet. Anil and Prakash started laughing very loudly.

Mayank - Idiots you both are. You made my pants dirty. What's this nonsense?

Anil (laughing) - It's okay yaar. Your own dirt is also a pure nectar.

Mayank - Then you should drink yours everyday. All your sins will be washed away.

Prakash - Oye! Stop fighting now you two. I can see a tap there Mayank, go and wash it.

Mayank - Yes. I'll go.
Mayank went to the tap but he couldn't open the tap. He tried a lot but when he put all his force, it broke. All the water started flowing from there. He got scared and started fixing the tap. Anil and Prakash were not aware of this as they were a little far and not noticing Mayank. One guy came there at that moment and quickly started fixing the tap with whatever things he could use which were lying there down. Mayank was shocked and surprised how he could fix it so quickly without using any equipment. But Mayank couldn't see his face clearly till now as he was busy fixing the tap. But the moment he got up, Mayank saw him and he kept staring at him for a few minutes. Anil and Prakash too noticed that guy and they were shocked.

Anil & Prakash - Oh shit! This is the same person.

Mayank - You are the same person right?

Boy - I'm Rajveer.

Mayank - Yes we were searching for you only.

Rajveer - We?

Prakash and anil reached there said we means we all. Then each one of them handshaked Rajveer and introduced themselves.

Rajveer - Hi! I'm Rajveer. But why are you searching for me?

Mayank - We want to talk to you. We need your help.

Rajveer - My help?

Anil - Actually we are searching for someone. But we can't find him. And we feel you can help us.

Rajveer - How can I help you?

Prakash - Wait. Let me show you a photo. Here it is.
Prakash showed him the photo and asked him whether it was him.

Rajveer - He looks like me. But this is not me. This guy has not even wore the glasses and I cannot even see without my glasses.

Prakash - He doesn't even wear glasses in real life, I mean he didn't used to. As far as we know. But his face resembles exactly like you.

Anil - That's why we came to you.

Rajveer - Do one thing. All of you come to my house. It's just the Opposite. We'll sit and talk there. You all look very tired.

Mayank - Yes. This is a good idea. Let's go friends.

When they went with him, the door was locked first and when they entered, they saw something unusual. Rajveer had lots of machines which they had never seen. They were all sensorized. All the machines operated on Rajveer's voice. There was a computer like a wall there which automatically got switched on when Rajveer entered the house.

Mayank - How did the computer get switched on?

Rajveer - Don't worry. It's not automatic. It scanned my eyes the moment I unlocked the door. That's why the machines started working.

Anil - Superb! I cannot believe that it's real.
After some time, there came a voice, "WELCOME SIR."

Prakash - From where did this voice come from?

Rajveer - This is the voice of my computer. He knows that I'm in the house now.
Anil - This feels like a lab yaar.

Rajveer - It's nothing so. I have done some small inventions. Anyways, you'll say. You were telling about some guy.

Prakash - Yeah. This is Raj's photo and we are searching for him for an important work. But we didn't find him. We found you who looks similar to him. So we came here to find out if you know anything.

Rajveer - See, I don't know any Raj. And I'm sorry. This picture is also not mine. I myself, I'm shocked that he looks exactly like me. I really can't believe it.

Prakash - We too sir. And now we can't really understand what to do.
Rajveer again took that picture in his hand and started laughing and said, "he looks almost similar to me."

Mayank - Yes. Difference is just the glasses and your hair is short.
Rajveer - I never thought anything like this is possible. But how can I help you now? I don't even know this person.

Anil - Are you sure sir, that you are not Raj?

Rajveer - Definitely not. What do you think I won't recognise my own photo?

Mayank - Sorry sir, he didn't mean it.

Rajveer - No. It's ok. I can't help you with this. But if you want any other help then tell me.

Prakash - No sir. Thank you. I think we should leave now.

Rajveer - May I know why you all are so curious to find this guy?
Then all three of them told him the whole story from the start. Rajveer understood their problem. He said, "I know yaar that the problem is too big but I think you only have to solve it on your own. And about the guy in the photo, who he is, where he is that I don't know."

Prakash - It's ok sir. No problem. We'll leave now.
When they were moving out of the house, suddenly Rajveer called them out,`` wait ".. Three of them turned back," there is one solution for this. "

Mayank - What is it?

Rajveer - I don't know about Raj but I can help you with this competition.

Anil - But how?

Rajveer - That you can see yourself. I have made this lab myself. And this talking computer too. I can do this for you. I can help you with your project work.
Mayank got happy. But Prakash and Anil still had some questions in their mind.

Prakash - But why will you help us?

Anil – Yes, How will it benefit you?

Rajveer - I don't have anybody else other than this computer to talk to. I'm alone. Just not me but you people also, will help me to get rid of my loneliness.

Mayank - Then you don't have to worry at all. Even devdas forgets his paro being with us and drinks alcohol happily. What say guys?

Prakash - If it's about helping, we are with you. You help us with our project.

Anil - Even I don't have any problems.

Rajveer - But I'll help you with one condition. Please don't call me sir, call me Rajveer. Do I look like an uncle to you?

Mayank - No man. You look younger yaar. And I guess we are simply giving you this respect. Our elders are also craving for such respect.

Saying this Mayank went to Rajveer and put his hand on his shoulders. Rajveer looked at him in rage and Mayank became numb.

Rajveer laughed after some time and then everybody started laughing.

Rajveer - That's like what I wanted. We are friends now.

They all hugged each other. And they said,"now we are a complete team."

They all sat down together and that time Anil asked Rajveer,

Anil - yaar, you are so talented then how come you are here?

Rajveer - This is my natural talent. Just like that. I like new new technologies. I just give tuitions to the kids. Make them aware about the technologies and practically teach them everything.

Prakash - You don't do anything else than this? Is this enough for your living?

Anil - Yes yaar. You are very talented.

Rajveer - Actually I like teaching people a lot. And the worst thing is I don't have any degree. And this world won't give me any job without it. Forget about the job, I won't even get recognition. But one day I'm sure of getting one. Just wait and watch.

Rest all were shocked that how this talented boy doesn't have any degree with him.

Anil - I cannot believe this yaar! Did learn this all on your own?

Rajveer - This is my passion. And I don't need a degree for that.

Mayank - And what about your family? Where is your mom-dad?

Rajveer - I don't have. My mom-dad expired in my childhood. I have an uncle who raised me up. But due to some work he is out now.

Anil - Then why didn't you complete your studies?

Rajveer - I had some family issues that made studying difficult for me.

Prakash - It's okay. You don't need to worry. You don't have to tell us everything. We can understand.

Rajveer - Thank you friends.

Mayank - Anyway, we have to go back to Mumbai now.

Anil - Yeah. God knows what's happening in college. We should be there.

Prakash - Yes. We'll leave tomorrow from here. Rajveer, can we stay here tonight if you don't mind?

Rajveer - Definitely! You can. Assume everything to be yours.

Mayank - Except underwear na?

All looked at Mayank in anger.

Prakash - Go run from here. Don't irritate us. Have you ever worn your own pants?
Rajveer started laughing listening to them.

Rajveer - Do you always be like this?

Anil - Always.

Mayank- I'll tell you something. This Anil has a secret crush on Prakash.
Prakash hit and told Mayank to shut his mouth.
Seeing all this, Rajveer started laughing out even louder. He could see his loneliness vanishing. He watched them doing stupid things for quite a some time. He was feeling relieved now.

Next Day Morning

Everyone was ready to go to Mumbai along with Rajveer.
Mayank - Ready, Rajveer?
Rajveer - What's there to worry when you all are there?

Anil - We should say this instead.

Prakash - Oye you all emotional party! Let's go. Don't want to be late.
Everyone was moving out from Rajveer's house. Rajveer put off all the machines. He took some of his files and his laptop along.
While going,

Mayank - Bye bye, talking computer. We'll miss you.

Prakash - Get going you joker!
All left from Raipur to Mumbai.

Mumbai

They all had reached their destiny, means in their dirty room in Mumbai.

Anil - So Rajveer, this is our Palace and from today yours too.

Mayank - This is good na?

Prakash - Stop your nonsense and contact Sharma sir. He might be in Nagpur or probably might have even reached. We will have to tell him that we didn't find Raj.

Anil - You are right.

Mayank - Oye, enter the house at least.

Anil - He is also right.
They entered the room. The room was fully a mess as usual. They said sorry to Rajveer for such a dirty room but assured to clean it soon.

Rajveer - No problem at all. I liked it.

Prakash - You don't have to worry. We'll clean it up right now. Mayank will do it for us. You rest for some time.

Mayank - Yes. Prakash you are right. Mayank will clean it all.

Prakash and Anil stared at Mayank.

Mayank - Wait a minute. I'm the only Mayank here. Idiot, Prakash. I won't leave you.

Prakash - Don't take tension bro. I was just kidding. We all will clean it together.
All three cleaned the room irritating each other. After cleaning, all four sat down together.

Anil - Finally this is done! Now what's next?

Mayank - Now we'll spoil it again.

Prakash - No jokes Mayank. We should think about project now.

Anil- yeah. Rajveer, what can we do for project? Do you have any ideas?

Rajveer - You people don't take any tension. I have an idea and I have studied on it yesterday in the train. Now I know what to present, I mean you three will.

Prakash - Oh god yaar! Thank you.. But what's the idea?

Rajveer - Do you remember my computer?

Mayank - Yes. That huge, Miss. Talking Computer.

Rajveer - Yes. That only. That is my idea. That computer has an operating system that controls all the machines connected to it. And basically it controls my whole room. We'll develop something similar here too.

Mayank - But that operating system is in your talking computer na? How will we get it here?

Rajveer - Don't worry. A similar OS, but a little specific operating system is in my laptop too. This doesn't control other things but it can do its work itself. Means, this computer like the bigger computer is self operated. But I need to work more on this as it cannot handle some commands in a proper way.

Anil - Meaning?

Rajveer - Means, it gets confused between my given task and his own task. For example, if I give him some task, it should follow my command but sometimes it gives priority to its own task.

Mayank - That means he is stupid and rude.

Anil - Shut up Mayank.

Mayank - Sorry.

Rajveer - Anyways, this is the problem. So it will take a little time as I will have to check its source programming and change a few things.

Prakash - No problem. We have a month for this.

Rajveer - There is nothing to stress about. I have only developed this operating system in both my computers. It was successful in the other one, so it should be in this too.
Prakash - but there won't be any problem in this project na? I mean, anybody else has not made it right or it's not a patent of anybody else na?

Rajveer - No. I have made it myself and I have an open source of this from where I can control it. May be big companies use these types of systems but this is not used by the public like Android and other smartphones. It can operate any system. Just imagine what all can happen with this.

Anil - And what about the disadvantages?

Rajveer - It will have. Of course. And which inventions doesn't have? Everything has its two sides. The things is how we use it.

Prakash - Ok done. Now we will submit this and represent this only.

Anil - Are you sure?

Mayank - Yeah. Think about it one more time.

Anil - What say Prakash?

Prakash - Ready.

Anil - Then me too ready.

Mayank - You are saying ready as if you are doing something on your own. I had asked to think once more to Rajveer not you stupid people.
Anil & Prakash - oh sorry. Rajveer, you only tell us.

Rajveer - I guess I'm ready. This is a chance for me to bring out my talent. All thanks to you guys.

Prakash - No Rajveer, Thanks to you. We didn't do anything. Get ready with the trophy Director sir, we are coming.

Rajveer - I have some work. I have to make a call. Excuse me please.

Mayank - Yes Bhai, sure.

Then Rajveer went to the balcony and stood there for quite a long time. God knows what he was thinking. Three of them started thinking what Rajveer was doing in the balcony for so long. So they went to him. As they went to the balcony, they saw Rajveer standing and was lost in some thoughts.

Mayank - What happened Rajveer bhai? Why are you not coming inside?

Rajveer - No yaar. Nothing. I just finished talking on the phone. It was a bit urgent. Sorry.

Anil - No problem yaar. Now go, get ready fast. We'll have today's food somewhere out.

Rajveer - Yes. Ok.
Rajveer went inside the room to change, and three of them were waiting for him outside the room.
When Rajveer removed his shirt, he saw the tattoos on his chest and back in the mirror. He stared at them and said to himself in anger.

Rajveer - Now just one more step and Director AJAY SHETTY my work is over. You will have to regret. I have reached very close to you now. Just one more step and you will have to accept your mistake.
All three were waiting for him outside.

Mayank - What has happened to this chashmish? Why didn't he come out yet?

Prakash - He'll come. Wait for some time.
Rajveer came out after some time and all went out to roam.

Next Day

Anil - Let's go to the college, bhai. We haven't been there for the last 4 days. God knows what's happening there.

Prakash(in sleep) - Oye! Why are you disturbing me? We'll go to college later. Let me sleep and you also go and sleep.

Anil - I haven't got up to sleep again with you stupid. Get up. We need to see what's the environment in college.

Prakash - You wake up Mayank first.

Anil - He woke up long back. He is working with Rajveer. Listening to this, Prakash woke up instantly and asked what Mayank is doing with Rajveer.

Anil - I think they are working on our project and Mayank is helping him with it. And I don't think Rajveer slept the whole night.

Prakash - Let's go and see them.
Anil and Prakash went to Rajveer' s room and saw Rajveer and Mayank working from outside.
Mayank was helping Rajveer with a serious mood even though he didn't know anything out of it,he was trying very hard.
Seeing this Prakash and Anil got happy and they went running and hugged Mayank.

Mayank - Aare! You both got up? I was here just so that Rajveer doesn't get bored.
They both kept hugging Mayank and Rajveer was standing right beside them.
Prakash saw Rajveer and called him near him and hugged him too.

Anil - Now let's go to college or not?

Prakash - Yes. I'll get ready fast.

Again College Days

They met Sanjay as they reached college.

Sanjay - How are you all? Is your work done?

Prakash - Yes yaar. Just got distracted a little.

Sanjay - Distracted means?

Mayank - Nothing much brother. It's a long story. Will tell you that later.

Anil - Tell us the status of the class first.

Sanjay - What has happened to you guys? You guys are so much interested to know about the class today. Did you fall sick coming from Raipur or what?

Prakash - No yaar. Just feeling that we should study a little bit now.
Sanjay started smiling listening to them and said that it's good that they are feeling so. And they went to the class.
And from that day, Anil, Mayank and Prakash started studying very seriously.

Prakash started studying mechanical along with sanjay very seriously, Anil in his electronics department and Mayank in his civil branch.

Three had started studying very seriously now and they used to understand everything practically whatever they learnt and used to discuss with Rajveer after coming home. They had started asking questions in class and even used to answer many questions too on their own.

Rajveer helped them a lot in their studies and he explained them things very clearly.
After college, they used to come and help Rajveer with the project. Their life had improved a lot. But they didn't stop having fun, irritating each other, and doing a lot of other mischief. And of course, they didn't even stop eating on the name of Sharma sir from the Canteen.
Slowly slowly, all four, Anil, Mayank, Prakash and Chashmish i.e. Rajveer had developed a strong bond. They used to spend their day well with each other. And yes, competition day was also coming closer with this all.

One day Prakash went to meet Sharma sir in college.

Prakash - How are you sir?

Sir - I'm good. I have heard that you people have got some boy to help you with the project. Sanjay told me that. But he is not Raj.

Prakash - Yes sir. We searched Raj a lot. But we didn't find him. But we found someone who looks exactly like him but wears glasses.
Sir smiled and said, "no problem. It's good till your work gets done. I just regret for not knowing where Raj is and what he is doing.

Prakash - But sir,I didn't understand one thing. We went to the address you gave us but that house was closed and the people staying nearby don't even know about Raj. Sir, are you sure that address was correct?

Sir - I also don't know Prakash. Nobody knows where Raj went and where he is. I gave you all the information I got. It's strange that you got another guy who resembles just like him.

Prakash - Yes. Just this one uses glasses.
They both laughed. Sir and Prakash were talking when one student came asking something to sir.

Student - Excuse me, sir.

Sir - Yes please. Tell me, what happened?

Student - Sir I wanted notes of thermo.

Sir - I had finished the concept of thermo long back. Why you want the notes now?

Student - Yes sir, actually I want the notes of just one week which you covered in class. Starting from 10th July.

Sir - Wait i'll give you.
Sir searched the notes and gave him.

Student - Thank you sir. I'll return them soon.

Sir - It's ok. Now you go.
Prakash was still sitting there.

Prakash - Sir, i'll also leave now.

Sir - okay. All the best for the competition.

Prakash - Thank you sir.

While he was going out, he just thought for a moment. Something came to his mind. On 10th July sir was with them leaving for Nagpur for 4 days. And taking one week classes was not possible. He thought how this could happen.

He thought a lot and immediately came back to the staff room but nobody was there.

He started checking out some files. He checked the register where he could find the proof that sir was in college from 10th July. He got the attendance file. He started searching for Deepak Sharma sir's name and checked July's list. He was shocked. He saw sharma sir's attendance was full from 10th july and he wasn't even absent on any day after that.

He couldn't understand anything. He thought again. "sir left for nagpur with us on 10th July. He reached nagpur on 11th July around 6 and were supposed to stay there for 4 days. Then how is it possible that its showing their presence here in attendance book for 11th July?"

Prakash went searching for the same guy who came for notes. Prakash came out of the staff room.

That time sharma sir saw him coming out but Prakash couldn't see sir and he went searching for that student.

On the one side, sharma sir went to the staff room and he saw that the attendance book is open with his name from July month. He understood that Prakash has seen and understood everything by now or may be he will know everything now.

On the other hand, Prakash was searching that guy. And he finally found him near the college garden. He stopped him and went to him.

Prakash - Wait, you just took notes from sir right?

Student - Yes. But what happened?

Prakash - Tell me confirm, did sir take classes after 10th July?

Student - Yes sir. That's why I went to take the notes as I was out and I had missed the classes.

Prakash - Can you show me the notes for a minute?
Student gave him the notes.

Prakash - Thank you.
He checked the notes standing there and saw there were all the notes from 11 July and further days too. He was shocked seeing this. He couldn't understand anything. He got confused. He returned the notes to the student, thanked him and told him to go. Prakash was unable to understand the things. He started doubting sir.
On the other hand, sharma sir called someone. He said, "there is one problem. We have messed up." and he narrated him the whole story.
There came a voice from the phone, "no problem. I think this is the right time. Whatever has to happen, will happen now only."

Sir - Okay. You take care.
And then sir kept the call.
Prakash went to Sanjay to solve the puzzle.

Prakash - Sanjay, tell me one thing, do you remember whether sharma sir had come to after 10th July?

Sanjay - I don't remember so much yaar. It's two months old story. How I'll remember so much?

Prakash - Yeah you are correct but I can't understand this.

Sanjay - What happened?
Prakash told him the entire story. From sir coming with them till nagpur, them searching for Raj everything.

Prakash - How can he be present on 11th July when he got down in nagpur for 4 days?

Sanjay - What's the problem in this? His work might have got cancelled. So he must have returned. What's there to think so much in this?

Prakash - No yaar. There is something fishy here. He was telling us about Raj the whole way and when we reached there, we couldn't find Raj anywhere. And when he was telling about Raj, I felt as if he knows everything about him and knows him very closely.

Sanjay - So what happened? See Prakash, you have to present your project in the next two days, so don't sit with unnecessary things in your mind. Are you understanding? Competition is in two days now, which is very important in your life.

Prakash - Competition! Yes Sanjay! Our names came automatically in the competition without we registering for it.
Sanjay - This is there! But what's the logic behind all this?

Prakash - There is something. Some logic behind this. Some connection. First trapping us in the competition, then knowing about Raj, we going to Raipur, not finding Raj, this is all connected.

Sanjay - Aare yaar! You are thinking all this unnecessarily. It was me who told you about Raj, remember? I guess I made a mistake by telling you this. You are simply stressing out.
Prakash - No yaar. It was about our career. We would have been destroyed. Somebody registered our name in the competition. None of the students can do this in the fear of getting caught. Then who can do this?

Sanjay - You please go home now and prepare for your competition. I don't understand this sharma sir. He is really strange. He told me to tell you about Raj first and then himself went with you people. Forget leave this all.

Prakash - One minute. What did you say? Sharma sir had told you to tell us about Raj?

Sanjay - Yes. Remember, I had come to the parking when you three were tensed. Before coming to you all, I had met sharma sir. He himself told me that you won't be able to handle the competition and tell you about our ex-student Raj who might help you all.
And then I came and told you people and also told you that he was removed from the college I guess because I knew a little about him.

Prakash - You knew? But how?

Sanjay - My brother was Raj's batch mate. I must have told u, I don't remember. I had heard about him so I told you a few extra things about him. But if sharma sir hadn't said, it would have not even struck me.

Prakash - Now I get it. Our names were registered in the competition. Then we got trapped in this Raj matter too. He himself disappeared telling us the whole story. Sending us to Raipur. But this story is not complete yet. There is a big secret behind all this that we should know.

Sanjay - If you are really feeling something wrong, then there is one way to find this out. My brother might be knowing something about Raj.

Prakash - This is the best option. Can you please call him now? Please.

Sanjay - Wait a minute. I'll call him right now.
Then sanjay called his brother who was in a senior batch in the same college.

Sanjay - Hello bhaiyaa! I wanted help from you.

Phone - Yes sanjay. How are you? Tell me what help you need. Do you want money or something?
Sanjay - I'm good bhaiyaa. I don't need money. Thank you. I wanted to know whether you remember Raj?

Phone - Who Raj?

Sanjay - Bhaiyaa. He was your batch mate. You had told me that he was an intelligent student
but he was removed from college for some reasons.

Phone - Oh. That Raj! I remember. But what do you want to know and why?

Sanjay - Nothing serious. I had some work to do. Please tell me something about him please.

Phone - Listen, he was my batch mate but our departments were different. I used to meet him sometimes. Yes, there is one thing, he used to always talk about developing a self operated system. He was very intelligent but something had happened when he was removed from the college. That's why I know about him. He was from IT department. I don't know anything more about him. And I don't have contact with any other student from our batch.

Sanjay - Ok no problem. Thank you, bhaiyaa.

Phone - It's okay,sanju. Yeah,one more thing. Is sharma sir still in the college? Deepak Sharma?

Sanjay - Yes bhaiya. But why did you ask?

Phone - He can tell you more about Raj. He is his uncle. You can talk to him if you want.

Sanjay (shocked) - What?? Sharma sir is his uncle? Bhaiya are you talking about Deepak Sharma??

Phone - Yes sanju you can talk to him.

Sanjay - Ok bhaiyaa. I'll keep the call. I'll talk to you later.

Phone - Ok fine. Take care.

Sanjay - Yes bhaiyaa.

Sanjay kept the call and was shocked listening to his brother. He told all this to Prakash.

Sanjay - You were right. Sharma sir is Raj's uncle. He has hidden many things and lied to us. You were right. There is something big behind this.

Prakash - What? Sharma sir is Raj's uncle?

Sanjay - Yes.
Prakash was very shocked hearing this. Now he had come
to know that all this was planned. Now the pages of the
story were getting connected.

Prakash - What more did your bhaiyaa say?

Sanjay - Nothing more yaar. They both were from different
branches so they hardly met. Oh yes, he said one more thing
that, Raj was very intelligent and he always spoke about
developing a self operated system. But he was removed out
of the college.

Prakash - What? Self operated system?
Now Prakash got more worried and thought that he has
heard about this somewhere. He could remember someone
telling him about self operated system. And his brain
worked. "this is Rajveer."

He started remembering all the things about Rajveer. All the
things that Rajveer said started revolving around his head
like, I haven't completed my studies, I have developed this
self operated system, I have an uncle but his out due to
some work...etc etc.

Prakash understood who Rajveer is. But he couldn't
understand why he did this all. He was very angry and he
directly ran to his house from there.
He told sanjay that he has some important work and left.

At Room

Prakash reached in the room.

Mayank - Prakash, you came? See this. Today we prepared our own food. Come on, let's have it.
Prakash - Where is Rajveer?
Prakash shouted in anger.

Mayank - What happened Prakash? Is there any problem!?

Prakash - Where is he? And where is Anil?

Mayank - Rajveer is inside the room. He is doing the final testing of our project.
Then Anil too came there and seeing Prakash he asked, "What happened? Why are you so angry?"

Prakash - Come with me you both.

Three went to Rajveer's room. Rajveer said looking at them, "how are you bhai log? your work is done, project is ready. now see, you all only will win."

Prakash - Why did you do so? How did this benefit you?

Rajveer - What are you saying? I didn't understand anything.
Prakash went in anger and pushed Rajveer towards the wall and he grabbed his neck and said," you have cheated us! "

Rajveer's glasses fell off his eyes as he was pushed and he couldn't see anything without them. Seeing this Mayank and Anil came running and held Prakash from behind and asked him what he was doing?

Mayank - What's wrong with you Prakash? Have you gone mad?

Anil - Oye! This is our Rajveer. What has happened to you?

And there Rajveer was searching for his glasses. He couldn't see anything properly. He couldn't even find his specs. Rajveer's eyes got wet and he asked, "where are my glasses? Please, give me my glasses."

Mayank gave him his glasses and asked whether he is fine.

Rajveer - I'm fine.

Mayank - Prakash, you did wrong to him. You have really gone mad.
Prakash - Friends. Don't be foolish. He is a cheater. And he is not any Rajveer.

Anil - What are you saying Prakash?

Prakash - You all want to know the truth na? This is not Rajveer. In fact, Rajveer doesn't even exist in real life. This boy is Raj only. Raj Sharma. And together with sharma sir, he has trapped us.

Mayank - This is wrong Prakash. Why are saying this? Don't be foolish.
Prakash - I'm telling you the truth. I have found it out just now. Sharma sir is his uncle. Director had removed him only 6 years back. He was a cheater then and now also he is a cheater.

Anil - This is all shit.

Mayank - Yes Prakash. Why will Rajveer trap us and for what reason?

Prakash - I also don't know about it. He will only tell us the truth today. Why he did this. One thing we know that he is

Raj Sharma. If you don't believe me, then ask him only. He is our friend na, he cannot lie now.

Rajveer - No. I won't lie. Not at all because I have been friends with you all. (Rajveer said in a low voice and almost crying)

Rajveer - You are right, Prakash. I'm Raj. But I didn't cheat anyone. Yes I have lied to you all. Took your help to reach here, to reach Director AJAY SHETTY. But I didn't cheat anyone nor I wanted to lie to you all.

I didn't even cheat then, nor will I now. I'll tell you the truth, the whole truth because you all have the right to know it. You all are my friends right?

PAST

Everything was going fine and it was our 5th semester in college. I and Srishti were very happy. And everywhere in college, there was an environment of BE - ENGINEER competition. I too had started working on my dream project, self operated system. I had thought about this on a small level, at that time. The way it is advanced now, it wasn't at that time.

One day Srishti told me that she wants to go to Delhi as one of her relatives was unwell. I had gone to the station to drop her.

Srishti - Raj listen, have your food on time ok. Don't be into your computer the whole day. Ok?

Raj - Yes baba. I will eat.

Srishti - Promise na?

Raj - Yes. Pakka promise. You too take care of yourself and come soon. I'm alone here.
Srishti - I'll come as soon as my aunts health is better. And listen, after coming I'm going to tell dad about you.

Raj - What will you tell Srishti? I'm not anything yet.
Srishti - I just want to tell him the truth. I don't want to hide anything. And anyways you are a lot… Topper, Intelligent and dad will like you.

Raj - I'm not a topper anymore. I was.

Srishti - Yes baba. After me. Chalo. Train has come. Take care of yourself. Bye….

Raj - You too. And I'll call you.
And then Srishti left.

After two days, it was BE - ENGINEER competition. And everyone was busy with their projects. I too was into my project and I had almost finished my work.
In the same competition, Director's son, Sunil also had participated. He too had made some high tech project. We had to give a brief presentation about our project on the day before the competition so that only selected people can go ahead.

We all gave our presentations one by one. Judges were sitting inside and only the one who had to present could go inside. And when it was my turn, I entered.

When I presented my idea and my project, all the judges liked it very much and they appreciated me and said that I will surely win.

After an hour selected candidate names were going to be announced.
And when the announcement was made, I couldn't understand anything. My name wasn't there in the announcement.

I was very tensed. I went to find out about this as I was very sure of getting selected. Noways my project was going to be rejected,that too in the selective test.

I went to the judges to inquire about this. This competition was from B-TECHNOLOGY and all the judges were also from the same company. When I reached near the judges,

Raj - Sir, excuse me?

Sir - Yes.

Raj - Sir, I want to know, why my project is not selected? I did the best I thought.

Sir - What is your name? Let me check.

Raj - Raj Sharma.
Sir check the results list. Raj's project was sealed with copied mark and was written as disqualified.

Sir looked at Raj with anger and said, "You cheat first and then come asking me for a copied project?"

Raj (shocked) - Sir I didn't copy any project. This is wrong.

Sir - Shut up and get out. Thank god that no action is taken against you yet. You know the rules
right? Cheating in this can throw you out of the college. Your career will be destroyed.

Raj - Please sir listen to me once. I have not done anything like this. This is wrong.

Sir(angrily) - I said get out.
Sir was not ready to listen to Raj. He shooed him away from there.
Then I thought I (Raj) should talk to Director sir. But when I reached there, I saw sir is already sitting and talking with the owner of B-TECHNOLOGY in his office. I heard some of their talks waiting outside the door. I felt as if they were talking something about me. I heard Director sir thanking B-TECHNOLOGY's owner.

Owner - What's the need to thank me for this sir? You got us here in your campus, you have given our education platform a chance, gave so much of money, have handled our shares. So we can definitely do this little thing for you.

Director - Yes of course. But in return, you too are taking good care of us. You didn't do any judgement for any student and disqualified them...

Owner - That was our plan to mark some projects as copied and some as failed and throw them out of the competition and make your son win the trophy.

I was listening to all this from outside and was shocked hearing this. Director had cheated on the students. He had bought B-TECHNOLOGY's shares and given money to the owner and made his son win the competition. So that his son gets rewarded with educational status. He wanted to give him everything that other students could achieve through their own talent.

B-TECHNOLOGY was a big company and worked on Engineering and Technologies education frame.

It was a big achievement at that time, to get certified from this company. And director sir had bought it all himself.

I went to meet director sir later. He was rounding up the college.

Raj - Sir, I want to talk to you.

Sir - Yeah, say.

Raj - Why did you do this? I have made the best project. You have cheated on all the students.

Sir - What rubbish are you talking?

Raj - I'm not talking rubbish sir. I have heard everything. You have cheated all the students
keeping this competition.

Sir - Oh.. So you know everything? But what can you do now? Tomorrow the winner will be announced and that will be my son.

Raj - This is wrong. I'll tell this to everybody.

Sir (laughing) - What will the students do? Do whatever you want to.

Raj - Sir, please don't do this. This is my dream project.

Sir - What's your name?

Raj - Sir, Raj Sharma.

Director - Oh.. You are the one who's name is Sealed as copied! Thank god, that nobody knows this and you are not getting any punishment. Now get lost from here.
Sir started walking out from there.

Raj said to sir from behind, "sir please, don't do this. This won't be right."
And director sir slapped Raj in anger.
Blood came from Raj's mouth and he had tears in his eyes.

Director - It will just take a minute for me to ruin someone like you. This is a good part of me, that I'm not doing it. Study quietly here, complete it, take the degree and get lost from here.

I came crying out from there.
Director then felt that I might create a problem later on. Students might come to know and it will create havoc. That's why Director seriously put a copied complaint on me, insulted me in front of the whole college and said that I copied the B-TECHNOLOGY's own project. And called me a theft. He accused me of this and B-TECHNOLOGY too supported him in this as they were

getting a lot of funds.
Everyone started looking at me in a weird manner, nobody spoke to me. Nobody used to like
me then. All said something or the other bad to me.

Srishti was still in Delhi. She knew nothing about this. I did not talk to her from past many days as I was broken inside. What would I tell her? That she is in love with a cheater?
If anybody was there then it was her only for me. She was everything to me. But I didn't want to

hurt her with this with what I was suffering.

Uncle helped me a lot. Made me understand. I told him everything what had happened but I knew that he too couldn't do anything about it.

One day I was sitting alone. Shattered and broken. I was crying a lot and all the things were running in my mind. I had seen my dreams break in front of my eyes.
I again went and tried to talk to Director sir.

Raj - Sir, I'm seriously not understanding what to do next. You have completely destroyed me.

Sir - For now I have just insulted you and not removed you from the college yet. You still have a chance. Complete your studies and get lost from this college.

Raj - No sir. Today I have not come here to ask you for anything,nor this system nor engineering. Because, staying in this system, if today I fail in it, one engineer will be finished and I wouldn't want it. Keep this system with you and take my advice. You change your engineering otherwise I promise to change your engineers one day. You cannot remove an engineer, now this engineering will be suspended. Wait and watch.

I said this all between my tears and my anger.
Director called for the security and shouted, "get out of this college, get out of my campus."
That time many of the students gathered there and there was a huge crowd. And then security removed me out of the college.

I came home and promised myself and my project that surely I will take the revenge of my dream. And it will be so big that the whole system will watch it and get my respect back. The respect which an engineer deserves, who hasn't stolen anything.

I could take my project anywhere, sell to the big companies but I wanted director to realise his mistake himself. I wanted to do something that would force him to approve my project and say that this project was mine that time and now too.

I tore my results that time itself as I didn't need them and came to Raipur leaving Mumbai.
Nobody knew me here. And uncle had his old house here so I decided to stay here.

PRESENT

Raj - So this is what had happened 6 years back. It was me who had hacked college server and panel and registered for you three.

It was only me who called you to Raipur, met you all myself, came back to Mumbai as I wanted to get my project approved from the Director Sir and wanted to prove that the charges put against me were wrong without looking into my project. I wanted to remove that.

I know I have done wrong, used you people, didn't tell you anything but what would I tell you? Please forgive me.

I was all alone after that incident. I needed a psychiatrist to handle myself, used to remember Srishti too a lot. I couldn't meet her after that, and can't meet also. What would I say to her?

She must have accepted this by now that I have cheated in the competition and on her too.
Raj started crying and begging for them to forgive him.

Mayank hugged Raj immediately and said, "You didn't do anything wrong yaar."
Anil - Yes yaar. Anyways, we were first only ruined but after you coming we got to know the true meaning of life. You didn't do anything wrong.

There were tears in everyone's eyes. Then Prakash came closer to Raj and hugged him crying and said," Please forgive me Raj. I was scared. I'm sorry. Please forgive me."

Raj - No problem yaar. We are friends and it's fine.(Raj had tears in his eyes at that moment)
Everyone had an emotional moment and tears saturated in their eyes.

Raj said after some time," I want to tell you something more, so please don't be shocked after listening to this."

Then Raj told them a big story after listening to which they had no choice but were shocked. What might it be?

NEXT DAY AT PROJECT PRESENTATION

Three of them did a lot of hard work and presented Raj's dream project with all their heart. They wanted to complete Raj's dream anyhow. They gave a fantastic presentation.
They had done this work very seriously. Guess they were never this serious in their entire life. But they gave their 100% for their friendship.

Director - Fabulous! This is a great project. How did you do this?

Mayank - We have a great friendship sir. So there wasn't a need to do anything else.

Prakash - Yes sir, we were together. So didn't realise anything.

Director - Good, I guess it was a success keeping this competition in groups.

Anil - Yes sir, we forgot all the engineering and became engineers ourselves and worked. That's
why this was possible.
After listening to this, director remembered all that Raj had said. But he didn't say anything about it.
He just said, "Congratulations. Your project is approved."

Three were very happy. They were happy that they were completing somebody's dream. They went to Raj running fast. They saw Raj standing far and had tears in their eyes.
They showed a thumbs up to Raj. Raj too started crying seeing them. He realised that the time has come for which he waited for such a long time.

He went and hugged all three and said thank you to them.

Prakash - Thank you for what yaar? It's you who did everything. We didn't do anything.
Mayank - Yes yaar. We were doing timepass all the time but you have made us worthy of something today.

Anil - And this Mayank was a big useless.

Mayank - Shut up. Now also you are useless and still have a crush on Prakash.
All started laughing then.

Prakash - Now just one work is left.

Mayank - What work?

Prakash - Tomorrow's day. I just hope that we win tomorrow. And then this story will come to an end.

Anil - Yes Prakash, you are right.

Raj - you all take care of yourself. Don't do anything that will trouble you later.

Prakash - Raj.. You don't take tension. Everything will be in front of people as soon as we win.
Raj looked at Prakash and smiled and said yes.

Next Day (Competition Results)

There was a big crowd of students in the college. Everybody's attention was on the competition today. What will happen and who will be the winner? Who's life was going to change today?
Today there was a different environment in college like a fair. Results were going to be announced soon.
Our three engineers also had reached college by now and Raj was at home.

At Room

Raj was sitting alone, quietly and he had tears of happiness in his eyes. He started talking to himself.

Raj - Today Rajveer is over Srishti, for ever. Today is the day to come in front of everyone. We have to tell the world the truth, the time has come.

Srishti, do you remember, I had promised you something once and you had ignored it as a joke? But now that is the truth and the world will see it today.

Now it's my turn to go. Now I'll go myself back to INSTITUTE OF ENGINEERING AND TECHNOLOGY, where we met for the first time, and from where this whole story had started, it will end there only.

I'm leaving Srishti, I'll go now.
And then Raj went from there.

On the other side in college,

AT COLLEGE

There was a crowd of some thousands of students in the college auditorium. Now the results were going to be announced.

The three engineers, Anil, Mayank and Prakash were holding each others hand and praying to the god.

Everybody's attention was on the announcement and the hearts of the contestants were beating very fast.

Director came on the stage along without senior faculty. He told some things, spoke for a few minutes and then the time had come for the announcement of the results. He took the mic and said,

" Today is a big day students but its not for those who are scared of this competition already but for those who had a lot of courage to participate in this. They have proved that

they are not weak and they have proved to be an engineer and I want you all to clap for them first. "
The whole auditorium clapped and there were very strong vibrations in the hall.

Director - Now without taking much time, I would like to announce the winners of the BE-Engineer competition.
All became silent and were waiting to listen to the name of the winner.
The breath of our three engineers was stuck as this was something more than a competition to them.

Director - And the winners of the BE-Engineer is the team, who made self operated system, the

Engineers- Prakash, Mayank and Anil.
Students clapped and this noise echoed the whole college. And Prakash, Mayank and Anil couldn't stop shouting out at the top of their voices. They shouted, screamed and jumped and hugged each other.
Sir called them on stage.
They came on the stage, they had tears in their eyes and even Sharma sir's eyes were wet. His naughtiest students had created a magic and the plan where he had helped Raj was successful today.

Three took the certificates and went towards the mic to say something.
Prakash took the mic and thanked everyone and said, "I want to tell you all something more important than this. It's not just me, but it's important for all three of us."

Prakash - We three friends, we just know how to enjoy and make fun. We are the idiots of Sharma sir but one day, someone made us realise what it is to be an Engineer. He made us realise that this engineering is our strength which says that we aren't any ordinary person. If you are together, then happiness is around and it feels alive.

We wouldn't have been here today in front of you all, if he wasn't there. Actually we don't even deserve this trophy. We have just done our part of work by completing somebody else's dream.
But by standing here today, I can see that, who's dream we have completed, has won today. Because I can see that he has completed our dream too along with his. Otherwise we would have been sitting somewhere like a useless and wouldn't have done anything. We had just entered engineering forcibly without thinking or having any passion. But he taught us the right meaning of engineering. We could see through his eyes that the support we have in this friendship, we won't find it anywhere else. Nowhere in this world. I'm proud of being an engineer today. Thank you. Thanks a lot.

Prakash became emotional saying this. Anil and Mayank kept a hand on his shoulder and consoled him. Prakash continued,
Until then people in the hall couldn't understand anything properly. But they were trying to understand Prakash and his friend's feelings.

Prakash - Sorry. Today is a big day which can make an Engineer cry.
I want to tell you all a small story. There was a very brilliant boy years ago. He was very intelligent. One day he made something and thought that the world will like it and he will get respect and gain fame in his life which we have got today. But one person broke his dreams and took away his happiness. Without seeing his talent and his abilities, he destroyed his life. And he was removed from this college in

a very bad manner and insulting him from the same competition 6 years back.

After listening to this, director sir understood everything and got to know that they are talking about Raj Sharma.

Prakash on mic - But that boy didn't become weak. He rebuilt his dream and completed it with the help of us three idiots.
He told us all the secrets he had but we were shocked listening to one. But we were proud of our friend and we will always be. Friends, this is not anybody else other than who made this self operating system.

Guys, please welcome, the one whom the world wants to know, whom nobody saw, and are in search, the founder of the WE-TECH CORPORATION.

Everybody was shocked and looking at the door as nobody had seen the owner of WE-TECH company yet. But everybody knew about WE-TECH as all had used the educational site of it.
Director and faculties couldn't believe that it is the same person and their eyes were on the door itself.

Nobody except the three and Sharma sir knew about this.

Prakash - Guys, please welcome, RAJ SHARMA, the founder and owner of the WE-TECH.
And then Raj entered the auditorium. All the people looked at him and students started pushing each other to get a sight of him. And here Director couldn't believe it, that Raj Sharma, whom he had removed from college is the founder of WE-TECH corporation.

People didn't stop clapping and all the faculties were shocked and they too couldn't stop clapping.

Students started shouting, "WE-TECH, WE-TECH"
Raj came on stage and hugged them. He said, "thank you guys, you have made it."

Anil - not us, we have made it.
They all smiled and then Raj went to the mic,

Raj - Please be quite friends. Thank you. Thank you so much for showing and giving your love to WE-TECH. Today it's all because of you that We-tech is such a big hit.
I had just promised once to someone that I would open a company for you. I'm upset that, that person is not here but I have completed that promise today. I want to apologise to her.
I'm sorry Srishti for not coming back. How would I come? I couldn't come with all those scars. All called me a cheater. I know I left you alone. Forgive me. I'm sorry. But believe me, there was not a single day that I didn't miss you.

Today I completed my work Srishti. Today I got my name back and my respect back.
There were tears in their eyes and even the students.
Raj - I know I haven't done anything big but just did my work. Work of being an engineer. And engineering doesn't mean having a degree. Everybody will have the degree at the end here but all won't be an Engineer.

I will request you all not to respect the degree but respect of you being an engineer. Don't let that name fall. That's it. This is all I want to say. Thank you.
All were quite listening to this. And then all were shocked seeing what happened next.

It was the director who clapped first and then everybody else followed.

Director came to Raj, he apologised to him and said, "You have proved that, You don't need a degree to be successful in life. I'm sorry. Forgive me for what I did. I'm proud of you. You are the true Engineer."

Raj - It is okay, sir.
Then Raj did another announcement on the mic.

Raj - Today I want to tell you something else too friends. Today, I give all the burden of WE-TECH to my dear friends, Prakash, Mayank and Anil. Now they are the part of WE-TECH.

Three were happy listening to this. All four were very happy that day. And they were lost in the noise of the claps in the auditorium.

Outside of College

Raj - Ok guys, now I guess I should leave.

Mayank - Where are you going?

Raj - It's time for me to go back. Whatever you guys have done for me, I'll always be grateful for that. And whatever trouble you have faced because of me, I'm sorry for that.

Prakash - Have you gone mad? If you say this again then I'll surely kill you.

Raj (laughing) - Okay.. I won't say.

Anil - but you can't go this way. We have thought something for you.

Raj - What?

Prakash - We have a gift for you. You remember you said you were alone? So now it's time to say bye bye to your pain.

Raj - I didn't get you.

Mayank - You'll get to know soon. Meet us at CST after some time.

At Chhatrapati Shivaji Terminus Station -

All four reached there.

Raj - what is there here?

Prakash - we told you na. We have a gift for you.
Mayank - you just come with us.

Raj - but where?

Anil - Aare! First sit in the train at least. Then we'll tell you.
All sat in the train.
Raj was still asking the same question, "where are we going?"
And three said, "you just come with us quietly."

After some time, they reached their destination. And Raj knew this place.
This place was Matheran, where he used to come 6 years back. And once he had got Srishti with him.
They got down from the train and Raj started looking at this place everywhere.

Raj - Why have we come here?

Anil - Because you are in need of coming here.
(Raj had got Srishti here when she was alone exactly 6 years back.)

Raj - But what will we do?

Mayank - The same thing that you should have done long back. But you forgot it yourself.

Prakash - Walk ahead atleast.
Then they went to the same place where Raj had taken Srishti on the same hill where it was surrounded with all the mountains.

Raj - You all knew about this?

Prakash - Of course. You forgot but we didn't. You remember, you used to say, let the pain of heart win over your mind and let that pain flow out. Who knows your life might change into something good? So it's your turn today.

Raj became very emotional listening to this. He was alone and he never thought he would feel good after coming there, where he used to come years back to get rid of his pain.

Anil - We all are with you today, Raj.

Mayank - Yes. Raj, remove all your pain out.

Raj - Why are you waiting then?
Then they faced the mountains and started screaming loudly. They all let their pain out and cleaned their heart.

Raj was very happy and he hugged them all.

They started walking back, and suddenly Anil, Mayank and Prakash said, "you sit in the train, we'll come soon."

Raj - Why? What happened?

Mayank - Aare. Go and sit na. We want to do susu.

Raj - Just now you all did it in the jungle. Now again?

Anil - We want to do it again. You sit, we'll come.
And then Raj went and sat in the train.

Train was almost empty. There were hardly anyone on the train. Raj went on a seat and sat. He was now feeling light. The burden he was living with had now vanished. Three friends had helped him come out of it. Only one thing was left, Srishti. He couldn't find Srishti yet.
Suddenly, a girl came in the train. Raj saw her, she was Srishti.

Raj was shocked seeing her. He couldn't say anything. He got up and went to her.
Raj had tears in his eyes and he said,

Raj - You? Here?
Srishti too was full of tears. She said, "I was here only. It was you who left me and went."

Raj - Forgive me please.

Srishti - No problem. But you became chashmish now.

Raj - You weren't there na, so I tried making six pack abs.
Srishti laughed hearing this.
Both had tears in their eyes and they cried looking at each other.

Then they both hugged each other and finally they both were together.

After that, the three engineers peeped inside the train and asked Raj, "so say Raj. Did you like our gift?"

Raj (smiling) - So, it's you three who did this?

Mayank - Why? What do you think? Only you can play games? Even we are engineers. Don't forget that!

Raj smiled and called them near him.

Raj - Thank you so much yaar, you got everything back to me. God knows what would have happened without you all.

Anil - Oye! Now stop your drama. Otherwise you know Prakash's attack na?

Then all four started laughing and Raj hugged Srishti and they were back together again.

Srishti - by the way Raj, what's this written on your hand in Chinese?

Raj – Raj & Srishti.

Three Engineers - Ohh..! Great.

Raj - Shut up you idiots.

And now what? Everything was fine now. Raj went back home with Srishti. Srishti told her dad everything and he was happy too. Our engineers started studying a lot and did a lot of masti too.

Director changed his education system. Now things didn't happen for degree there. He understood now, that a student like Raj is important.

Thank You

After 2 Years (2019) :

Our engineers have completed there engineering and after a long time they decided to went out togther and one day…

Our engineers were again peeing together on a playground. But Mayank was just acting of doing susu. When Anil and Prakash got busy peeing, Mayank slowly came behind and pushed them both and ran laughing from there.

Anil & Prakash - Oye! Donkey! You spoiled our pants.

Mayank (While running) - You remember na? Self dirt is a pure nectar. Had fun?
Prakash went to the nearest grossery shop and asked for the water.

Prakash after washing his hands.
Prakash to shopkeeper: Give me a paper, I don't have handkerchief.

Shopkeeper is finding for a rough paper and suddenly prakash take a newspaper placed over the desk of shopkeeper.
Shopkeeper- That is todays news paper.
Prakash- so what? Seat silently otherwise I will clean my poty and gift you the paper back.

Prakash took the paper and start tearing it but stopped when he saw a news on it.

News written on it: Wife of We-tech CEO RAJ found death in the home, Police is searching for the suspect whose name is Aman also known as **DARK.**

Prakash called mayank and anil shoutly .

To be continued...

The series followed by Next story

DARK: The Story of Blacknight (2020)

CEO will return
CEO: Rises Against The System (2021)

THE END

LOTS OF LOVE TO *MUMMAA...*